Bake

MW01134024

Leighann Dobbs

This is a work of fiction.

None of it is real. All names, places, and events are products of the author's imagination. Any resemblance to real names, places, or events are purely coincidental, and should not be construed as being real.

More Books By This Author:

Lexy Baker
Cozy Mystery Series
* * *

Killer Cupcakes
Dying For Danish
Murder, Money and Marzipan
3 Bodies and a Biscotti
Brownies, Bodies & Bad Guys
Wedded Blintz

Blackmoore Sisters
Cozy Mystery Series
* * *

Dead Wrong
Dead & Buried
Dead Tide
Buried Secrets

Contemporary
Romance
* * *

Sweet Escapes
Reluctant Romance

Dobbs "Fancytales"
Regency Romance Fairytales Series
* * *

Something In Red
Snow White and the Seven Rogues
Dancing on Glass
The Beast of Edenmaine

Chapter One

"According to Chef Dugasse, your pie crust is too thick," Lexy's assistant Deena said as she fitted a sheet of dough into a pie pan taking care to flute the edges the way Lexy had shown her.

Lexy glanced up at her as she worked the marble rolling pin over the dough, pounding it a little harder than necessary.

"I don't think *Chef* Dugasse knows his pie crusts," Lexy replied pushing down the anger she felt and wondering for the umpteenth time why she had agreed to fill in as pastry chef at the rustic lakeside resort.

When her grandmother Mona Baker, or Nans as Lexy called her, had phoned with the offer, it *had* sounded like fun ... at first. The current pastry chef had been taken ill, they were desperate for a temporary replacement—and they were willing to pay very well for it.

Still, Lexy wasn't sure why she had accepted. She had her own bakery to run where *she* was the boss and didn't have to listen to a pompous overpaid head chef berate her baking. But the promise of a free two week vacation in a rustic cabin with her fiancé, Jack, had won her over ...

... And she had regretted it every day since.

"How's this?" Deena stood back, indicating the pie plate.

Lexy tilted her head, inspecting the work. Deena had a part time job in the kitchen for the summer and Lexy had been training the enthusiastic teen on various baking techniques. Deena reminded Lexy of herself at that age—full of energy and eager to learn everything about baking. Training her was one of the few things she'd enjoyed about the temporary job and Deena was turning out to be a quick study.

"That looks great." Lexy squatted down so that her eyes were level with the table, then turned the pie plate and pointed to one section. "It's a teeny bit higher here."

Deena looked at the pie plate from table level and nodded. "Oh yeah. I can see that from this angle."

Lexy shrugged. "It just takes practice. You did a really good job for your first try."

Deena beamed with pride. "Thanks. If you ask me, Chef Dugasse is just being a jerk. Your pie crust is delicious."

Lexy agreed. Chef Dugasse *was* a jerk. He had been a thorn in her side since she took the position. She wasn't the only one that thought so, either. Most of the staff was at odds with him and it was no wonder with the way he was always yelling and screaming at them.

But he was world renowned, and his food was excellent, so he could do as he pleased and the resort kept him on.

Lexy glanced around the kitchen. The resort itself dated to the 1940s, but the kitchen had been recently renovated. Billed as a rustic-campy get away with five star dining, the meals had to be cooked to perfection so the kitchen, which sat inside a gigantic antique log cabin structure, was top notch.

It would be a pleasure to work in it ... if it wasn't for the domineering presence of Chef Dugasse.

Dugasse's voice thundered from the other side of the kitchen as if sensing Lexy's thoughts. "Theeze eggs are not up to our standards! You vill throw them out and start over!"

Lexy turned in the direction of the screaming. Dugasse was in a white chef's outfit complete with a tall hat. His six foot frame carried a three foot wide body, his gigantic bulk towering over a terrified first year cook, Thomas, who cowered in the corner. She watched as the head chef picked up the warming tray full of scrambled eggs and dumped them in the trash, then stormed off toward the back door that led outside.

Lexy saw Sylvia Spicer, Dugasse's long suffering sous-chef, rush over to soothe the cook's ruffled feathers. Sylvia's eyes shot daggers at the retreating back of the head chef before she started toward the door after him.

Lexy turned back to Deena who was still looking in the direction of the cook, wide-eyed with terror and her heart clenched for the poor girl. Lexy didn't see why Dugasse had to run the kitchen this way, almost everyone was terrified of him and it created an unpleasant work environment.

"Uh hum ..."

Lexy turned toward the throat clearing noise to find one of the chefs, Brad Meltzer, standing next to her. Brad worshipped Dugasse and the head chef often took advantage of that by sending Brad to do his dirty work, which Brad appeared to delight in.

Brad was as thin as Dugasse was wide. He had narrow, beady eyes and a pointed face which made Lexy think of a weasel. He didn't seem to like Lexy very much, which was fine with her since the feeling was mutual. Lexy raised an eyebrow at him.

"Dugasse says you have to make the cornbread for the *Chili Battle*." Brad jerked his head toward the back of the room where Dugasse had just disappeared.

"Excuse me?"

"The *Chili Battle*. They have it every year and it's a huge deal. The winner gets their own chili label to be sold nationally in grocery stores. Everyone knows Dugasse has a prize winning chili recipe so he's a shoe in. But he needs a cornbread side and that's where you come in."

Lexy felt her cheeks growing warm, anger causing her pulse to pick up speed. Having your own chili label was worth a lot of money, not to mention the branding opportunities for the chef. But she didn't see why *she* should have to put in extra hours to help make *him* rich and popular—not someone as mean spirited as Dugasse. She was sure he wouldn't do the same to help her if the tables were turned.

"That's not part of my job. I'm up to my eyeballs in pies and desserts here. I don't have time to make cornbread so that Dugasse can win some contest." She punctuated the chef's name by slamming her palm on the counter a little bit harder than she probably should have.

Brad's eyes grew wide. He took a step backwards and spread his hands at his sides. "Hey, I'm just the messenger."

Lexy swiveled her head toward the back of the room. Dugasse wasn't there—he must still be outside.

"Sorry, Brad. I know that. But I'm sick and tired of being bossed around by Chef Dugasse." She spun on her heels and started toward the kitchen door. "And I'm going to put a stop to it once and for all."

***

Lexy felt the eyes of the entire kitchen staff drilling into her back as she stormed over to the door. A blast of cold air from the giant freezer that stood next to it did nothing to cool her anger as she ripped the screen door open and stepped outside.

It was still early in the morning, but the heat of the day was starting. Lexy's hands clenched at her sides as she stood just outside the door ready to lay into the head chef.

Where was he?

Her eyes darted around the area, her heart pounding with anger. Straight ahead the woods full of tall pines was empty except for birds and squirrels. Normally, Lexy would delight in watching them scamper and fly about, but this morning she was too mad to notice.

To her left was a short path that led to the parking lot, to her right the dumpster, surrounded by the stench of rotting food.

Did he go somewhere with Sylvia? She'd thought she had seen the sous-chef head out here after him, but where could they be? Lexy cocked an ear to listen for their voices but didn't hear anything except the flies buzzing around the dumpster.

Tentatively, she picked her way around the end of the large metal container. She peered around to see if they were on the other side, her breath catching when she saw a pair of chef's clogs. But instead of the soles lying flat on the ground, they were sticking up as if the person were lying down.

Lexy raced to the other side of the dumpster. Her heart lurched up into her throat when she saw what lay on the other side. Chef Dugasse, lay on the ground—a big, shiny mahogany handled chef's knife sticking straight up out of his chest.

Lexy threw herself down beside him, her anger at the chef forgotten. "Chef Dugasse?"

No response.

Her mind whirled. What should she do? Should she pull the knife out and try to stop the bleeding?

Lexy realized she should check for a pulse. She placed her fingers on his neck.

Nothing.

She bent over him, putting her ear to his mouth to see if she could hear him breathing.

Nothing.

She tried his wrist.

Nothing.

Lexy sat back on her heels with a sigh, realizing there was nothing she could do.

Chef Alain Dugasse was dead.

***

A scream pierced the air, interrupting Lexy from digging her cell phone out of her pocket. She whipped her head around to see Sylvia

Spicer standing just behind her, hands over her mouth, eyes wide.

"You killed him!" Sylvia rushed over to Dugasse's other side, slapping his face and lifting his arm.

"What? I did *not* kill him. I found him like this." Lexy narrowed her eyes at Sylvia who had given up on the face slapping and arm lifting and was now staring at her over the chef's body.

"Where were you?" Lexy asked.

"Me? I was in the kitchen." Sylvia turned her attention back to the chef. "Should we hide the body?"

Lexy stared at the sous-chef as she pulled out her cell phone. "Hide the body? We can't do that. We have to call the police."

"Right, of course, I don't know what I'm saying." Sylvia pushed herself up and backed away from the body as if she just realized what it was.

Lexy made the 911 call while Sylvia paced back and forth, a whiff of musky perfume teased Lexy's nose every time the sous-chef walked by.

"Did you kill him?" Sylvia asked after she had hung up the phone.

"No. Of course not." Lexy studied Sylvia's worried face as she paced back and forth, wringing her hands. "Did you?"

Sylvia stopped and looked at Lexy. "Me? I wasn't even here."

"But I saw you come out after him." Lexy gestured toward the dead chef. "Right after he reamed out Thomas about the eggs."

Sylvia's brow wrinkled and she shook her head. "No, I didn't. I was in the freezer, cooling off. I was really mad so I went in there otherwise I *might* have killed him."

Lexy's teeth worked her bottom lip. She *could* have gone into the freezer, it was next to the door. And Lexy hadn't actually seen her come outside.

"But you have blood all over your shirt." Lexy pointed to Sylvia's chef's coat which was smudged with red. *Had it been that way before she knelt next to the body?* Lexy couldn't remember, she had been too distracted.

"So do you." Sylvia nodded at Lexy's shirt. Lexy looked down and her heart froze. She *did* have blood all over her—much more than Sylvia.

"Well, of course I do. I bent over him to see if he was breathing."

14

Sylvia stared at her. "Well, if you did kill him, you did all of us a favor."

Lexy rolled her eyes in exasperation. "I didn't do it."

Sylvia looked off toward the road as the sound of sirens split the air in the distance.

"Well, I don't care whether you did or didn't kill him, but my advice would be to get your ducks in a row."

"Why is that?" Lexy wrinkled her forehead at the other woman.

"Because I don't think the police are going to be very understanding when I have to tell them that I came out here to find you leaning over a dead body with blood all over your shirt."

Chapter Two

It didn't take long for word to get around and the kitchen staff crowded outside to see what was going on. Lexy was doing her best to keep them back from the crime scene when the police arrived.

"What's going on here? Don't you people know this is a crime scene? Haven't any of you ever watched TV?"

A short, round man flashed a badge and the crowd parted to let him and his entourage through. He stopped short when he saw Lexy and Sylvia with their matching blood stains.

"And who might you be?" He ping-ponged his dark eyes between the two women, his brows slightly dipped in a question.

Lexy stepped forward and introduced herself, Sylvia followed suit. The man's handshake was firm. He introduced himself as Detective Payne and the man beside him as his associate, Detective Wells.

They made an odd couple. Wells was over six feet tall, where Payne must have been only five foot six. Wells looked to be in his late twenties, Payne nearing sixty complete with partial balding and a protruding stomach. Wells looked professional in a dark blue tailor-made suit. Payne looked like a dork in a light blue polo shirt, and blue and red plaid Bermuda shorts.

"So you two found the victim?"

"Not me. She did." Lexy's stomach lurched as Sylvia pointed to her.

Payne swiveled his eyes toward Lexy. "So that's how you got the blood on you?"

"Yes. I saw him lying there and rushed over to see if I could do some sort of first aid. I must have gotten the blood on me then." Lexy's stomach churned as she looked down at her shirt.

"Hmm ..." Payne cut his eyes toward Wells, then walked back to the edge of the dumpster and looked at the kitchen door. "So, why were you out here, on this side of the dumpster?"

"What?" Lexy furrowed her brow at him, then remembered why she had walked around the dumpster. "Oh, I came out looking for the chef."

Payne raised his brows. "Do you normally find him behind the dumpster?"

"No." Lexy bit her lip. This wasn't going good. Maybe she should stop talking now, before she got herself into trouble. "I thought he would be just outside the back door. But when I didn't see him there, I peeked around and that's when I saw his shoes."

Payne scrunched up his face and walked over to the kitchen door. He made a big show of looking around, then came around the side of the dumpster.

"Oh yes." He nodded, pointing the pencil he held in his hand at the shoes. "They stick right out."

Lexy did a half smile and nodded as Payne came back over to them.

"And you?" Payne fixed his attention on Sylvia. "How did you get the blood on you?"

"I came out and saw chef on the ground and ran over to him to try to revive him. I didn't realize that Lexy had already determined he was dead."

Payne looked up at the sky, pursed his lips together and tapped them with the eraser end of the pencil.

"Yes, but what made *you* come all the way over to this side of the dumpster?"

Lexy saw a cloud pass over Sylvia's blue eyes and her brows wrinkle slightly. "Well ... I ..." She looked toward the door, then back at the body. "I came outside to have a word with Chef Dugasse and heard the commotion over here, so naturally I came over to see what was going on."

Commotion? Lexy didn't remember making any commotion.

Someone jostled Lexy's elbow—apparently a crime tech who was trying to do their job of cataloguing the scene. It was getting crowded around the body and Lexy shuffled closer to the dumpster to give them room.

Payne looked around, wrinkling his nose as if suddenly becoming aware of the crime scene investigators swarming the scene and the stench of the dumpster.

Payne pointed to Lexy and Sylvia. "Let's finish this inside," he said jerking his head in the direction of the kitchen. He turned and started toward the door, almost tripping over an investigator that was scouring the ground for evidence. Wells fell in step behind him.

Lexy exchanged a raised eyebrow glance with Sylvia and followed them inside. The kitchen staff, who had been gathered in a circle, quickly dispersed to their various stations as soon as they entered the kitchen. Lexy realized that with Dugasse gone, Sylvia was now in charge.

Payne rambled over to the least crowded spot in the kitchen—the table where Lexy had been rolling the pie dough—and leaned against it. Wells stood to the side as if awaiting orders.

Payne looked down at a small spiral bound flip pad he had taken from his pocket when they were outside.

"Now, where were each of you when the murder happened?" Payne poised his pencil above the paper and widened his eyes at Lexy.

"Oh, I was right here. I was rolling pie dough and I saw chef over there." Lexy pointed to the end of the kitchen where she had seen Dugasse yell at Thomas. "Then I saw him go outside. I didn't go out until a few minutes later and found him with a knife in his chest."

"And someone saw you here?"

"Yes, several people. My assistant Deena and another chef, Brad."

Payne scribbled on the pad, then turned to Sylvia. "And you?"

"Well, I'm not sure exactly when he was murdered, but I went over to Thomas after Dugasse yelled at him, then I went into the freezer for a few minutes. When I went outside, he was already dead."

Payne's eyebrows mashed together. "Who is this Thomas?"

"He's one of our cooks." Sylvia looked around the room, then spotted Thomas by the sink and pointed him out to Payne. Payne gave Wells a slight nod and the other man headed off toward Thomas, presumably to harass him with his own line of questioning.

"And why was Mr. Dugasse yelling at him?" Payne pronounced the chef's name as de-gassey and Lexy stifled a giggle.

"It's pronounced *doo-gah-say*," Sylvia said.

Payne made a face. "What?"

"The chef's name. It's pronounced *doo-gah-say*," Sylvia repeated, then continued. "He didn't like the eggs Thomas had prepared, thus the yelling."

"And did this chef yell a lot?"

Lexy and Sylvia both nodded.

Payne looked up at the ceiling and tapped the eraser end of his pencil on his lips. "So, would you say he was unpopular?"

Lexy and Sylvia nodded again.

"And who would have wanted him dead the most?"

Lexy looked around the kitchen. The rest of the staff, who had been craning to hear what was being said, suddenly developed a keen interest in their various tasks. She felt a shiver run down her spine. The head chef had just been murdered, yet everyone was going about their business as if nothing had happened. Then again, the resort couldn't shut the kitchen down. The meals were included in the price for paying guests so the food service had to continue uninterrupted.

No one liked the recently departed chef, but would anyone here have disliked him enough to kill him? She turned to look at Sylvia. If they didn't bring in anyone from the outside to replace Dugasse, she'd benefit the most. *Was a head chef's position worth killing over?*

She shrugged. "No one really liked him that much, but I don't think anyone here would kill him."

Payne tapped his pencil on his lips while he looked around the room. He narrowed his eyes at Lexy and Sylvia, his gaze moving to their bloodstained shirts.

"You were both out there with the body. Either one of you could have had time to thrust the knife into the chef ... or both of you together. It only takes but a second."

Lexy's stomach dropped, anger flaring at the detective. But then she realized he was only drawing the logical conclusion ... she'd probably think the same thing herself. Except she knew that *she* didn't do it. Sylvia, she wasn't so sure about.

Payne twisted his face into a grimace, making exaggerated sniffing noises. "What is that smell? Is something burning?"

Lexy sniffed. She *did* smell something burning. She whipped her head in the direction of her ovens, her heart clenching when she saw smoke streaming out of them.

"My pies!"

She ran to the ovens and jerked the doors open. A dark cloud of smoke billowed out. She shoved her hands in some oven mitts and batted at the smoke. Choking and coughing, she reached inside the oven and brought out twin flaming pies.

She dumped the pies in the sink, running water on them to douse the embers.

"You bake the pies?" Payne gestured to the other pies on the counter, the ones that weren't blackened hunks of coal.

"Yes, I'm the pastry chef here." Lexy tore off the oven mitts and tossed them on the counter, her spirits sinking. She'd have to work fast to get the right number of pies out in time for dinner and Payne was taking up valuable time.

"What kind of pies are these?"

"Huh?" Lexy scrunched her face at the detective who gestured at two of the pies she had finished earlier which were cooling on the counter. "Apple and blueberry."

"And this one?" he asked pointing to one in the back.

"Lemon meringue." Lexy wondered what this had to do with the dead chef.

Payne tapped his lips with the eraser end of his pencil. "May I?"

Lexy's brow creased deeper. Was this guy for real? He wanted a piece of pie? Now?

She nodded slowly.

Payne reached over and grabbed a chef's knife, cutting a large slice of pie. He looked at the knife as he pulled it out.

"This looks similar to the knife that killed your chef." Lexy's stomach clenched as Payne turned his dark eyes on her. She glanced over at her knives, her shoulders relaxing when she realized they were all there.

"Well, all my knives are accounted for, so it wasn't one of mine that killed him." She nodded toward the knife rack on the counter, then remembered the mahogany wood on the handle. "Besides, that knife had a mahogany handle ... mine are rubber."

Payne narrowed his eyes at the knife, then grabbed a plate from a stack of clean ones beside him and plopped the pie on it. His eyes darted around the counter, looking for something to eat the pie with. Lexy held out a plastic fork hoping to speed up the process and get rid of him.

"Mmm...'s good," he mumbled around mouthfuls. Lexy shuffled her feet impatiently.

"Detective ... the murder?" Wells appeared at Payne's side, eyeing the piece of pie he was demolishing.

"Right," Payne said, swiping a gob of meringue from the plate with his sausage-like finger and then licking it off. He put the plate down and consulted his flip pad.

"Chef Dugasse was murdered." He announced the obvious, looking up from his pad. "And someone in this room is most likely the killer."

All work in the kitchen ceased. All eyes turned to Payne.

"How do you know that?" Lexy asked.

"Well, you all had opportunity." Payne looked around the room. "Since you were all here in the kitchen, anyone could have slipped out to do the killing."

"But what about motive?" A voice from the other side of the kitchen cut in. Lexy cringed, recognizing the voice as her grandmother's. It would be just like Nans to run on down here upon hearing there was a murder. Her grandmother had an odd hobby. She investigated murders and, judging by the gleam Lexy saw in the older woman's eyes, she was right on top of this one.

Payne's eyes lit up. "Very good Ma'am. Who here wanted the chef dead?"

His question was met with silence.

"No onc? You all loved the chef?"

Most of the staff looked down at the floor, some shuffling their feet and many of them murmuring, "no".

"You all didn't like him, then?"

Lexy saw Brad step forward. He gave her bloody shirt a pointed glance.

"Some of us liked him, but many didn't. Especially her." Lexy's heart lurched as Brad pointed straight at her. "In fact, right before Chef Dugasse was murdered, I heard her say she was going to put a stop to being bossed around by him *once and for all.*"

Chapter Three

It took an eternity for Payne and Wells to leave. The short detective bombarded Lexy with a series of questions, then warned her not to skip town before demanding her blood stained chef's shirt as evidence.

Lexy glared over at Brad who watched them with a satisfied smirk on his face before she changed her shirt and put on one of the kitchen aprons.

Somewhere in the middle of questioning Nans had left, but not before demanding Lexy's presence once she was done with her baking. Her grandmother seemed practically giddy with delight and Lexy figured she'd probably have the large rustic cabin she shared with two of her friends turned into some sort of command center to use for running the investigation by the time she got there.

Lexy got busy rolling out dough. She needed twenty pies for the dinner service and all that questioning had taken up valuable pie-making time. She worked at breakneck speed since she didn't want to waste the whole day in the kitchen.

"I can't believe Brad ratted you out like that," Deena said, cutting her eyes toward Brad.

Lexy pursed her lips. "Yeah, what a jerk." Then looking up at Deena's wide eyes, she added, "I didn't kill him."

"Oh, I know that," Deena said, then leaned across the table and lowered her voice. "Do you think it was someone in here?"

Lexy glanced around the kitchen. Sylvia had easily slipped into the role of head chef and was overseeing the food preparations. She had to admit that Sylvia was much more pleasant than Dugasse. Could she be the killer?

Everyone else seemed to be focused on their job. No one was acting like they had just stabbed someone.

"I don't know. The police seemed to think so, but it could have been anyone, really."

"Yeah, someone could have come from the woods and killed him. I bet a guy like that had a lot of enemies," Deena said as she turned to put two more pies in the oven.

Lexy glanced out the kitchen window at the large section of woods behind the dining lodge. Someone *could* have come from the woods. There were several paths out there.

"I heard he was behind the dumpster. What was he doing there?" Deena started pouring the filling into more pie shells.

Lexy bit her bottom lip. "I don't know."

What *was* he doing behind the dumpster? She'd assumed the chef had gone out for a smoke, but usually the smokers stayed right outside the kitchen door. There would be no reason for him to go behind the dumpster ... unless he was lured there or had some sort of secret meeting and didn't want to be seen.

Lexy finished rolling out the last of the pie dough, cut it into two circles, and quickly fitted them into pie plates for Deena to fill.

"Can you fill these and bake them, then set them to cool? I need to take off," Lexy said as she untied her apron.

"No problem." Deena nodded, getting to work with the pie filling.

Lexy bunched up her apron and threw it in the clothes hamper as she headed toward the door.

She was in a hurry to get to Nans. This case had a lot of angles to it and she'd feel much better if someone competent was looking into it. She didn't know if she trusted the pie eating Detective Payne, but she *did* know that Nans and her friends were good at solving crimes. They'd even helped the police department back home—where her fiancé, Jack, was a homicide detective—solve several cases.

Plus, she figured, it couldn't hurt to do some investigating of her own. It might help solve the case more quickly and she wanted to make sure the real killer was caught ... especially since *she* seemed to be the one that was at the top of Payne's suspect list.

***

Lexy stopped outside the dining hall, taking a deep breath to calm herself from the stresses of the morning. She was no stranger to dead bodies. In fact, she seemed to come across them frequently, much to the dismay of her fiancé ... and the delight of her grandmother. But still, it was never pleasant to find someone dead ... or to become the number one suspect.

Starting down the hill, she tried to push the image of Chef Dugasse with a knife sticking out of his chest from her mind. Instead, she focused on the scene in front of her.

The dining lodge was at the top of a hill with panoramic views of the rest of the resort. Lexy looked out over the pristine lake which was dotted with kayaks and canoes. Sunlight glinted off the deep blue waters. The peaceful sound of chirping birds filled the air and the smell of pine permeated her nostrils adding to the tranquil scene.

The resort was all about nature and relaxation. The roads were dirt, more like paths and people rarely drove cars on them—only to get to their cottages and to leave the resort. Most people walked or drove small golf carts inside the complex and the absence of the drone of car engines added to the peaceful feeling.

Quaint, rustic cottages painted in reds, blues, whites and greens—their shutters with cutouts of pine trees sat along the roadways. Most of them had porches complete with rockers and the yards were bursting with colorful displays of flowers. Lexy could see hammocks swinging in the breeze and wished she had time to relax in one.

Turning left on Aspen Lane, she headed toward Nans' cottage which was one of the largest in the resort. It sat at the very end of the street and had a huge front porch on which Nans and her three friends, Ruth, Ida and Helen were waiting.

"Lexy, are you okay?" Ruth hugged her.

"Come inside dear, we made some tea." Helen held the door to the cottage open and ushered Lexy inside.

"Tell us all about finding the body." Ida scooted a chair out from the wide pine table that sat next to a large window on one side of the room, indicating for Lexy to sit.

Ruth appeared at her side with a steaming cup of tea and then all four ladies took their seats around the table, staring at Lexy with wide, excited eyes.

Lexy sipped her tea and looked around the room. It resembled the squad room from an episode of *Castle*. There was a giant white board with a picture of Chef Dugasse on it and different columns of information. Papers were piled up on a nearby desk. Nans' iPad was charging on the coffee table.

"Where did you guys get that?" Lexy waved at the white board.

"Oh, Norman brought us to Staples and helped us with it," Ida said referring to her fiancé who had accompanied her on vacation. They had a small cottage near the lake while Nans, Ruth and Helen shared this one. Lexy and Jack had their own cottage a few streets over, which they shared with Lexy's white Poodle mix, Sprinkles.

The thought of her dog made Lexy smile and she glanced at her watch. She'd better hurry, she wanted to take Sprinkles for a walk before dinner and she should spend some time with Jack ...

"Tell us everything you know about the murder." Nans interrupted Lexy's thoughts.

"There's not much to tell. I went out to talk to Chef Dugasse—I had seen him go outside earlier. When he wasn't outside the door, I looked a little further and I saw his shoes on the other side of the dumpster, toes up. I ran over and there he was with a knife in his chest."

"You didn't see anyone else, or hear anything?"

Had she?

"I'm not sure, I was so distraught at finding him like that, I really wasn't thinking."

"So he was already dead?" Helen went over to the white board.

"Yes, I think so."

"And what time was that?"

Lexy gnawed on her bottom lip. "I'm not sure, I didn't look at my watch or anything, but it was probably about five or ten minutes before I called 911."

Lexy pulled her cell phone out of her pocket and looked through the sent calls. "The 911 call was sent at eight twelve."

Helen wrote the time on the white board.

Nans got up from her chair. "So, you went out the door and looked for the chef?"

"Yes, I already said that."

Nans held up her finger. "When you didn't see him, you looked around the dumpster." Nans mimed looking around an imaginary dumpster in the middle of the room.

"Yep." Lexy nodded.

Helen scribbled something on the board.

"Then you saw his shoes and ran around to the other end of the dumpster?"

"Yeees ..."

Nans ran around the imaginary dumpster, threw her hands up in mock surprise and then knelt on the ground. "Like this?"

Lexy nodded and sipped more tea.

Ida went over beside Nans and looked down at the imaginary body. "You checked his pulse—he was dead. What else did you do?"

Lexy shut her eyes, trying to remember exactly what happened. "I checked his pulse—his neck and wrist and then I leaned over to see if he was breathing ... and that's when Sylvia came out."

"Sylvia, the sous-chef?" Ruth wrinkled her brow at Lexy.

Lexy nodded.

"She was out there?" Ruth asked.

Lexy nodded again.

"Won't she get the head chef position, now that Dugasse is dead?"

Another nod.

"Then she could be our killer!" Ruth went over to the white board and added Sylvia's name under the 'Suspects' column.

"Which direction did Sylvia come from?" Ida asked

Lexy pursed her lips. "She came from behind me ... I didn't see exactly where, but I assumed she came out the kitchen door."

"But she could have been hiding on the other side of the dumpster after killing the chef," Nans said.

The ladies murmured their agreement.

"She had means, motive and opportunity!" Helen punctuated the last word by jamming the cap onto her white board marker.

"Well now, let's not get too excited," Nans said. "We can't call the case closed without doing a proper investigation."

"Right." Helen took the cap off her marker and posed her hand over the white board. "Who else do we have for suspects?"

Everyone looked at Lexy.

"What?"

"Who else would have wanted your chef dead? Did he have enemies?" Nans asked.

"He was mean to everyone in the kitchen, but I don't think that would be a reason to kill him ... unless he really pissed someone off. He *was* yelling at Thomas right before he was killed but Thomas didn't leave the kitchen." Lexy's eyebrows mashed together. "But I did see Sylvia heading toward the door after the chef."

"Aha! So she *was* out there," Helen said.

"Well, she said she was in the freezer. The freezer door is next to the door that leads outside. I didn't actually see her open either of the doors." Lexy shrugged.

"But she could be lying," Nans pointed out.

"Sounds like we'll have to do some digging to see if anyone besides Sylvia would have had motive." Ida picked up the iPad and powered it on. "Are there any surveillance cameras in the kitchen? Ones we could use to see exactly where Sylvia *did* go?"

"I don't think so. The kitchen is pretty old and low tech. But I can ask Thomas, he might have seen where she went," Lexy offered.

"What about the murder weapon?" Ruth asked.

"It was a standard chef's knife," Lexy said. "Thankfully all of mine are accounted for, plus the handle on that knife was different from mine."

"*Yours* are accounted for, but were anyone else's missing?" Nans wrinkled her brow at Lexy.

"I don't know." Lexy bit her lip trying to picture the kitchen. Most of the chefs had their own personal set of knives, too bad she hadn't thought to look to see if anyone was missing one.

"You should check that out tomorrow," Ruth said. "In the meantime, we'll see what we can dig up online about Chef Dugasse and ask around about any potential enemies."

"What did you think of the detective in charge of the case?" Nans turned to Lexy.

Lexy made a face. "Not much. He seemed more interested in eating pie than finding the killer ... which he seemed convinced might be me."

"Well, don't you worry. We'll find the real killer in no time, isn't that right, girls?" Nans turned to Ida, Ruth and Helen who all nodded.

Lexy stared at the four women, their cheeks flushed with excitement. She had to hand it to them. They were in their 80s and still sharp as a tack. With several successful investigations under their belts, they'd had great success solving murders back home. They'd even given themselves a name—*The Ladies Detective Club*.

Lexy felt a momentary pang when she realized this was supposed to be a vacation for them and she was causing them to have to work when they should be relaxing on the beach.

"I really appreciate you guys doing this, but I don't want to ruin your vacation," Lexy said taking her tea cup to the sink.

The ladies looked at each other and Nans spoke. "Don't be silly. Vacations are nice and all, but to tell you the truth, we were getting kind of bored."

"Yeah, we need to keep our brains active," Ruth said.

"Who wants to lie on the beach when we could be tracking down a killer?" Ida rubbed her hands together.

"That's right," Helen said. "Now you run along and let us get to work."

Lexy felt her shoulders relax. She smiled at the women. "Thanks, I *do* feel a lot better knowing you guys are on the case."

She was in the middle of hugging them when the chirping of birds erupted from her pocket. She dug out her cell phone and her heart clenched. It was Jack.

She'd been dreading explaining the morning's events to him. He took a dim view of her getting mixed up in murder cases, and they'd had more than one fight over her investigating cases with Nans and the *Ladies Detective Club*. This time she was going to have to put her foot down.

She was a prime suspect and didn't want to depend on the bumbling Detective Payne to find the real killer. She hated to do anything that would jeopardize her vacation with Jack ... or their engagement ... but she was determined to investigate this one with Nans and the ladies, whether Jack wanted her to nor not.

Chapter Four

"... and I seem to be the prime suspect." Lexy studied Jack's handsome face as she steeled herself for a lecture on the dangers of getting involved in murder investigations.

She felt her brows knit together as Jack smiled at her. He'd listened patiently while she'd relayed the morning's events, including the part about how Nans had turned her cottage into a crime investigation center. She'd expected him to be mad, but he was sitting there as calm as could be, changing out the reels on his fishing pole.

"So, you don't trust this detective ... what's his name?" Jack asked.

"Payne. Do you know him?"

As a homicide detective himself, Jack knew a lot of the other detectives in the state. Lexy was hoping that if Jack knew Payne, he might be able to get some information on the investigation.

Jack shook his head. "Never heard of him. But if you and Nans are on the case, I'm sure you'll ferret out the real killer."

Lexy stared at him. "You're not mad?"

"Why would I be mad?"

Lexy narrowed her eyes. "Usually you get mad when I get involved in these types of things with Nans."

Jack put down his fishing rod and came over to her, putting his hands on her upper arms.

"Lexy, I've come to realize that you're going to do what you are going to do no matter what I say. I can't fight it. So, I'll just have to trust that you won't do anything dangerous." He put his thumb on her chin, tilting her face up to look at him. "Right?"

"Right." Her heart melted at the look of concern in his eyes. He bent his head, brushing his lips against hers and her stomach flip-flopped. She snaked her arms around his neck, pressing herself against him.

"Woof!"

Her dog, Sprinkles, jumped at her leg, stealing her attention from Jack. Lexy reluctantly released Jack and bent down to pet the little dog who was pawing at her calf.

"Hi Sprinkles. You want to go for a walk?"

The dog barked, jumped in the air and spun around.

46

"I guess that's a yes." Jack laughed. "Let's leash her up and take her out. I have a few hours before evening fishing."

Lexy crossed their small cabin and picked Sprinkles' harness and leash off the hook by the door, then put them on the small white dog which was quite a feat considering that Sprinkles was wiggling and jumping the whole time.

"Where do you want to go?" Jack asked.

"Well, if you don't mind, I wanted to check out the trails behind the dining hall. Payne thinks the killer was someone in the kitchen, but the murderer could have come from one of those trails. There are several that lead right to the dumpster area."

"So you're thinking Dugasse might have had a rendezvous with someone, or he was lured back there?" Jack opened the cottage door for Lexy and Sprinkles tugged her outside.

"Exactly." Lexy's heart soared. Jack seemed eager to help with the case which was a huge win for both the case and their relationship.

"Okay, let's take this trail." Jack indicated a trail next to their cottage that led up the hill and Lexy started toward it.

Sprinkles led the way, prancing eagerly up the path, stopping every so often to sniff something. Lexy was grateful for the tall pine trees that provided a cool respite from the hot afternoon sun. She breathed in the thick woodsy smell, watching the chipmunks scurry through the leaves. Her flip flops slapped the backs of her heels as they navigated the path.

She'd walked this path before, but she'd never really paid attention. She looked at the slats of sunlight that filtered through the trees and realized the whole forest was a warren of trails.

"There's so many paths, the killer could have taken any of them."

"True, but the trick is finding which one is most likely. That's assuming the killer did use one of the trails to make his getaway."

"Well, what do *you* think? If this was your investigation, what would you do?"

"The paths are one angle to investigate. But I'd start where I always do—with the family." Jack glanced at Lexy. "Did Dugasse have a wife?"

"I'm not sure." Lexy pursed her lips trying to remember if she'd ever heard of a wife or any other family.

"Well, if he did, that's a good place to start. Then find out if he had any enemies, look into his finances. That's all pretty standard, I'm sure Nans has that covered." Jack smiled down at her.

They walked in silence for a few minutes, stopping with Sprinkles whenever she found something interesting to sniff or wanted to mark her territory. Lexy wondered how the dog seemed to have an endless supply for territory marking.

Lexy could see a small clearing up ahead. "Isn't that the dining hall?"

"Yeah, let's check it out."

Lexy turned in that direction and Sprinkles was only too happy to lead the way, her nose twitching in the air as she smelled the aroma of roasting meat from the kitchen.

Lexy stopped at the head of the path. She could see the dumpster about twenty feet away, roped off by yellow crime scene tape.

"So, that's the scene of the crime," Jack said it as a statement.

"Yeah, he was lying right there." Lexy shivered and Jack put his arm around her.

"I'm sorry you had to find him like that. It must have been awful for you."

Lexy shrugged. "Well, it wasn't fun, but I guess I must be getting used to finding bodies since it didn't affect me nearly as much as the others."

Jack cocked an eyebrow at her but didn't say anything.

Lexy looked around the area where four paths met. "So, Detective ... which path is the most likely?"

"Well, the path we just came on leads out to the street near our cottage. The killer could have run down the path and no one would have noticed." He pointed to the path across from them. "That one goes parallel to the parking lot, I think."

"Yes, and you can see most of it from there, so the killer probably didn't take that one. Plus you have to go past the kitchen door and someone would have probably noticed him."

"That leaves these two paths here." Jack pointed to two trails that forked off deeper into the woods.

"I don't know where those go. Should we take one?"

"Well, if I was running the investigation, I'd have my people scouring each path for evidence." Jack frowned at the crime scene tape over by the dumpster. "But it looks like Payne is only searching the dumpster area."

Lexy's brows knit together. It seemed like Payne wasn't even covering the basics. Another reason to investigate it herself.

"Do you know if he had his people look at the paths?" Jack asked.

"I don't know but I can ask around. Maybe I will suggest it to him."

"Yeah, I'm sure that will impress him," Jack said dryly, then started down one of the paths. "Let's take this one and see where it leads. Keep a close eye on the ground and see if you can pick out anything unusual."

"Unusual? Like what?"

"A button, a scrap of paper, a shoe print. Anything that wouldn't naturally be there."

Lexy followed him down the path. She stared at the ground looking for a clue which was difficult with Sprinkles pulling her this way and that. After a few minutes, they came to a dead end.

Lexy's stomach dropped.

"That's it? The path just ends?" She looked around for another path, but found only thick woods—too thick to walk through.

"I guess the killer wouldn't have taken this one." Jack shrugged and started back the way they had come.

"If he did take a path, then it must have been the fourth one," Lexy said.

Jack stopped and looked at his watch. "Maybe, but I need to get back and get my fishing gear ready to go fishing this evening. I don't think it's a good idea for you to walk that path alone this close to dusk. Maybe we could walk it another time?"

Lexy felt her back go stiff, her shoulders tense. She hated being told what to do, but Jack was right. It probably wasn't smart to follow the path a killer might have taken alone.

Jack pulled her over to him. His right hand massaged her neck, melting all the tension she had felt a moment ago.

"Besides..." His left hand traced the waistband of her shorts. She sucked in a breath, her stomach tingling as he pulled the shorts away from her stomach just an inch and peered down. "I was hoping to get a look at your tan lines before I head out."

Chapter Five

Lexy woke up early the next day. She had to make five batches of brownies and several dozen cannoli and she wanted to get a head start. Plus she wanted to get in early to get a good look at the knife situation.

She entered by the dining hall front door, then went through the double stainless steel doors that separated the dining room from the kitchen. The doors opened to the end of the kitchen opposite from her baking station. Taking her time walking down the middle, she glanced around at each chef's station feeling more disappointed the further she went. It looked like all the knives were in place.

Donning her apron, she gathered, flour, cocoa, eggs, salt, vanilla, sugar and butter and brought them over to the giant mixer on the counter. Unlike her bakery where she usually made small batches, the dining hall was set up to feed large groups of people at once. The kitchen was used for cooking in bulk and she could mix gigantic batches, then pour several pans of brownies and bake them at once.

Deena came in just as Lexy was measuring the last of the ingredients into the gigantic mixing bowl.

"Is that for the brownies?" Deena stood on her tiptoes to peer into the bowl.

"Yep. I came in a little early to get things started." Lexy turned on the mixer. "But this will work out good because we can put the brownies in the oven and then get straight to work on showing you how to roll the cannoli shells."

Lexy felt a smile tug the corners of her mouth when she saw the teen's eyes light up. She remembered back to when her biggest worry was learning to roll the thin pastry correctly, unlike today when she had to worry about things like being arrested for a murder she didn't commit.

Lexy checked the mixer to make sure everything was mixed thoroughly. The smell of chocolate wafted up and her stomach nagged her that she hadn't eaten breakfast. She shut the mixer off and wrestled the bowl out of the stand.

"I'll pour and you can hold the pans."

Deena grabbed the side of an oversized brownie pan while Lexy struggled with the heavy bowl, somehow managing to pour the batter in without dropping the whole thing. They repeated the process for four other pans, then Deena ran them to the oven which Lexy had already preheated.

Lexy turned toward the fridge, intending to get the cannoli dough she had made the day before and bumped right into Thomas.

"Oh, sorry—I didn't see you." She put her hand on his arm to steady herself. "I hope you are doing okay after … you know … yesterday."

"Oh yeah. That was disturbing." The young man stepped back from Lexy, his eyes darting around the kitchen.

"Yes. Well, chef didn't have any right to yell at you like that."

Thomas' face turned red. "Surely, you don't think that I … I—"

"Of course not." Lexy interrupted him. "I know you didn't even leave the kitchen. But I was wondering …"

Thomas raised his brows at her.

Lexy leaned closer to him and lowered her voice. "Did you see where Sylvia went after she talked to you?"

Thomas wrinkled his face, sucking in his bottom lip and running his teeth over it. "I don't remember. I don't think I was watching her ... I was too busy trying to get more eggs made for breakfast."

"Oh. Okay, thanks," Lexy said.

Thomas nodded and scurried off. Lexy continued on to the fridge. She let out a sigh as she searched for the dough. If Thomas didn't see where Sylvia went maybe someone else did. But who?

Deena was waiting at the table when Lexy returned with two balls of dough. She handed one to the teen. They floured the table and their rolling pins, then started rolling the dough.

"You didn't happen to notice where Sylvia went yesterday ... after that whole incident with Thomas, did you?" Lexy asked.

Deena stopped rolling, her brow creased in concentration. "No, I wasn't looking that way. But I think my friend Jules was over near there. I can ask her if you want."

"That would be great." Lexy felt her heartbeat pick up speed a notch. She remembered being a teen and how they used to gossip about everything going on in the kitchen. The teen network here could be a valuable resource and she had an "in" with Deena. "Actually anything you can find out about that day ... or Chef Dugasse would be helpful."

"Okay, sure. I'll ask around." Deena looked up from rolling the dough and whispered, "On the sly."

"Thanks," Lexy said, giving her dough one final pass with the rolling pin.

"I like to roll the dough about one eighth inch thick." Lexy held up the edge of her dough as an example. "That will make the shells nice and crispy."

Deena nodded rolling her dough to the same thickness.

"Okay, good." Lexy grabbed a round stainless steel cookie cutter from a drawer and handed it to Deena. "Now cut the dough with this ... that will make the shells."

Deena pressed the cookie cutter into the dough, cut a circle, then placed it down again as close to the previous cut as possible so as to make the most use of the dough they had rolled out. Lexy felt a swell of pride—she'd taught her well.

Lexy cracked an egg into a little bowl and beat it with a metal whisk, then added a teaspoon of water and beat it some more. She grabbed the cannoli form—a round stainless steel tube that was about one inch across.

When Deena was done punching out the dough, Lexy picked one of the circles up.

"Okay, this is easy. You just take the dough and wrap it around the cylinder." She wrapped the dough so just a tiny piece of the edge overlapped.

"Then you take the pastry brush, brush some egg wash on the edges and press them lightly together so it doesn't come unwrapped when you fry it." She illustrated with the brush then handed the form to Deena.

"Now you try it," Lexy said.

Deena gingerly picked up a form, then a circle of dough. Lexy watched her wrap it, a little off center but still not bad for a first try. She was dipping the brush in the egg wash to help wet the edges when she heard a familiar voice behind her.

"Looks like we're having cannoli for dessert!" Nans navigated the kitchen, carefully stepping on the rubber mats. Ida, Helen and Ruth followed along behind her.

"Hi!" Lexy greeted the ladies. "What brings you here?"

"Oh, you know, we were in the neighborhood ..." Nans gave the kitchen a sweeping glance, then leaned in toward Lexy and lowered her voice. "We were wondering if you made any progress."

Lexy frowned. "Not really, but I'm working on it. Do you guys want some brownies? I'm just about to take them out of the oven."

Nans held her hands at chest level, palms out. "None for me, thanks."

Ruth, Ida and Helen shook their heads. Lexy narrowed her eyes at them. It wasn't like the ladies to turn down a dessert.

She left Deena to the cannoli shells and went to the oven. She was bent over, trying to lift the large pan out when she sensed someone behind her. Straightening, she spun around, her heart jumping when she saw Brad standing there.

"Can I help you?" she asked in a not very friendly way.

"I see you're still here even after yesterday," he said.

Lexy put her hands on her hips, anger pulsing in her veins. "And why wouldn't I be?"

"Well, it's just that it's awfully suspicious that you stormed off after chef yesterday and then he ends up dead ... with his blood on your shirt." Brad glanced over toward her knife set.

"Yes, my knives are all there," Lexy said taking the brownie pan out of the oven and slamming it on the counter. "So my knife was *not* the one that killed Dugasse."

"Really?" Brad raised an eyebrow at her. "It sure seemed like you were mad. And you had the opportunity. You could have used any of the knives from the kitchen ..."

Lexy ignored him, turning back to the oven.

Brad glared at her. "What's a'matter? Don't have a snippy answer for that one eh?"

"Don't you have some work to do?" she shot over her shoulder.

Brad started toward the front of the kitchen then turned back to Lexy. "Enjoy what time you have left in the kitchen ... I heard Payne is here and he might be ready to make an arrest."

Lexy's heart clenched. Surely Payne didn't have any evidence to arrest her with?

"What was that all about?" Nans stared at Brad's retreating back.

"I have no idea. Yesterday he made a big deal out of telling Payne that I had stormed out after Dugasse vowing to stop him once and for all ... or something like that."

"And did you?"

Lexy cringed. "Well, I guess I did ... but I didn't mean I was going to stop him by killing him!"

"Oh, so you didn't kill him?" A voice behind Lexy made her jump and she whirled around coming face to face with Detective Payne in a white polo shirt and a new pair of plaid Bermuda shorts—these in purple and yellow.

"No. I. Did. Not," Lexy said, taking another tray of brownies out of the oven and slamming them on the counter.

Payne's eyebrows went up. "Are these brownies?"

"Yes."

He rubbed his hands together. "Are you going to cut them?"

"Yes."

Payne grabbed a plate from the stack near the sink and held it out to Lexy who felt her mouth hanging open. Was he serious? She was about to give him a piece of her mind when she remembered Nans' old saying about catching more flies with honey then vinegar. Maybe if she kept giving the detective pastries, he wouldn't want to arrest her.

She took the plate, grabbed a knife—not a chef's knife like the one that killed Dugasse, a smaller one—and cut neat rows in the pan. Then she removed an extra-large brownie, put it on the plate and handed it to Payne, forcing herself to smile in the process.

"So, Detective ... what brings you here? Do you have more questions?" Lexy asked after he'd taken a few bites and mumbled his approval.

"Mmmm ..." Payne put the plate down and blotted his lips with a tissue he took from his pocket. "Yes, of course. I did come here for a reason. It seems some new evidence has come to light."

Lexy's stomach clenched. "It has?"

"Yes." Payne turned to face the rest of the kitchen and raised his voice. "There is a new suspect ... someone who has been seen sneaking up to the kitchen on several occasions."

The kitchen grew silent, everyone stopping their tasks and turning to look at Payne. Lexy's heart thudded with anticipation.

"And that person is in the room right now." Payne slowly looked at everyone in the room, his pencil poised in the air as he surveyed the area.

"Who is it?" someone asked.

"It is ..." Payne suddenly stopped, then whirled in the direction of Nans and her friends. He stabbed his pencil out toward them.

"Ruth Weston!"

Chapter Six

Payne's words hit Lexy like a punch in the gut and she whirled around to look at Ruth along with everyone else in the kitchen.

Ruth's hand fluttered around her throat, her face turning an unhealthy shade of red.

Nans, Ida and Helen all said "Ruth!" at the same time.

Lexy turned back to Payne. "That's got to be some sort of mistake. Why would Ruth be sneaking up to the kitchen?"

"It is no mistake. I have it on good authority." Payne picked up the plate and shoved the rest of the brownie in his mouth.

Lexy narrowed her eyes at the room wondering who would have said such a thing. Her gaze came to rest on Brad who was leaning against the sink, arms crossed on his chest, a smirk on his face.

"Ruth, tell him that's not true," Nans said.

"I ... well ... I can't," Ruth stammered.

"What? Why can't you?" Nans asked.

"Because," Ruth looked down at the floor, "it's true."

"What?" Ida gasped. "But why would you be sneaking around here?"

Ruth's chest heaved as she took in a deep breath. She looked up at Nans. "I was sneaking rolls."

"Rolls!" Helen said sharply.

Ruth's face turned even deeper red.

Lexy's brow creased. "Why would you have to sneak up to the kitchen for rolls?"

"Oh, it's this darn Paleo diet. It's killing me!" Ruth said.

"What? What Paleo diet?" Lexy cut her eyes to Nans.

"We've been on the Paleo diet. You know eating like a cave man? It's supposed to be very good for you and help slow down aging. God knows we can use all the help we can get in that area," Nans said.

"So, we're sworn off baked goods. We agreed to eat only meat, fruits, nuts and vegetables. Didn't we Ruth?" Helen turned to Ruth whose face got even redder.

That explained why they didn't want the brownies, Lexy thought.

"But what's that have to do with Chef Dugasse?" Lexy asked.

"Nothing," Ruth said. "I didn't even know the chef. I was just sneaking over for rolls. Jules would give them to me."

Lexy looked at Payne. "This seems pretty flimsy. Why does that make Ruth a suspect?"

"My source told me she was very sneaky like she didn't want to be seen. In my book, that's suspicious."

"Well, maybe Jules can corroborate Ruth's story."

"Which of you is Jules?" Payne bellowed out into the room.

A young, blonde girl stepped forward, her eyes flitting around the room.

"I am," she squeaked.

Payne made circling motions with his pencil. "Well, tell us. Did you give Ruth the rolls?"

"Yes, she came the past three mornings. Early. Said not to tell anyone."

"And did she fraternize with Chef Dugasse?"

"No, sir." Jules picked at the strings fraying from her apron pocket. "She just poked her head in the door and asked for a couple of rolls and some butter."

"At the back door?" Payne pointed his pencil to the door that led out to the dumpster.

66

Jules nodded.

Payne turned to Ruth. "And did you see Chef Dugasse ... or anyone else out there?"

"No." Ruth shook her head.

Payne looked up at the ceiling, tapping the eraser end of his pencil on his lips in the familiar gesture that Lexy took to mean he was "thinking".

"What time was this?" he asked.

Ruth glanced at the other ladies. "I wanted to eat the rolls and get back before Helen and Mona got up so I always came at seven thirty on the dot."

Payne did more pencil tapping on his lips. "The medical examiner places the time of death between seven forty-five and eight fifteen. So that would be too early to kill the chef ... unless you lurked around the dumpster, killed him and then went back to your cottage."

"That's impossible." Nans cut in earning a raised eyebrow look from Payne. "We have our alarms set for seven fifty am prcciscly and Ruth was already there when mine went off. So she wouldn't have had time to kill the chef and get back to the cottage."

Ruth turned to Nans, Ida and Helen. "I'm so sorry if I let you down. But I just couldn't go without bread!"

Helen grabbed her hand. "That's okay, Ruth. To tell you the truth, I snuck a Mounds bar the other day."

"I ate some animal crackers at the beach," Nans added.

"And I snuck one of Norman's scones," Ida confessed.

"Ladies! Ladies!" Payne waved his arms. "Let's stick to the morning of the murder."

Nans, Ruth, Ida and Helen turned their attention back to Payne.

"Now, you came from the parking lot to the back door?" Payne asked.

Ruth nodded.

"You didn't come up the path by the dumpster?"

"No."

"And did you see anything unusual while you were there?"

Ruth scrunched up her face. "I'm not sure this has anything to do with your investigation, but the parking lot is usually quite empty at that time of morning ... except yesterday there was a very unusual car in the lot. It stuck right out.

Payne made impatient circling motions with his pencil. "Are you going to tell us what it looked like?"

"It was a pink Cadillac. I've never seen one before. It was quite striking."

"Who here has a pink Cadillac?" Payne said looking around the room.

No one fessed up.

"No one knows who owns such a car?"

Everyone shook their head. Payne scribbled in his notebook. Lexy tapped her foot impatiently.

"Are we done here?" Lexy asked.

"Not quite ..." Payne eyed the brownies.

"But Ruth is free to go, right?" Nans asked.

"Yes, I suppose she is in the clear," Payne said reaching into his pocket and producing a business card which he handed to Ruth. "If you remember anything else that might be useful, give me a call."

Ruth took the card and the women started toward the door with Nans miming instructions to Lexy to meet her at their cottage when she was done.

Lexy tried to go back to cutting the rest of the brownies only to be interrupted by the annoying detective.

"I do have some bad news for you," he said to Lexy. "Sylvia Spicer says she found you standing over the body so if there's anything you want to tell me ..."

Lexy felt her cheeks grow warm, she glanced over at Sylvia her stomach tightening with anger.

"Why would I kill him?" She turned back to Payne. "If you ask me, Sylvia had more of a motive—with Dugasse gone, she gets promoted to head chef ... and *I* saw *her* heading in the direction of the door right before I went out and found him dead."

Payne's brows shot up, he scribbled in his book. "She said she was in the freezer."

Lexy shrugged. "Well wouldn't you say that, too, if you didn't want to be suspected of murder?"

Payne tapped the eraser on his lips. "Yes, I guess I would."

He reached over, took another brownie and then started in the direction of the door. After taking two steps, he turned around jabbing the brownie in her direction.

"I still have more clues to put together, but I'd say it doesn't look so good for you. I've done some digging and I know you've been involved in other murders."

Lexy started to protest and he held his hand up to silence her.

"I know, you were never charged with any of them, but it seems rather suspicious to me that you're always around when a dead body shows up." He leaned in toward her, his dark eyes drilling into hers. "I'm going to be looking into you very carefully. Rest assured that if you had something to do with *this* murder, your detective boyfriend won't be able to get you out of it this time."

Chapter Seven

It was noon by the time Lexy and Deena stuffed the last cannoli shell with her sweet ricotta recipe. She threw her apron into the bin, said good-bye to Deena and grabbed a cannoli on her way out the door.

She took the same path to Nan's cottage as she had the day before. This time she was more focused on the sweet creamy pastry than the scenery. The hours spent over the Fry-O-Lator had paid off. The shell was perfectly crunchy. They were sure to be a big hit at tonight's dinner. Speaking of which, Lexy realize she'd better hurry if she wanted to have some beach time with Jack before they had to come back to the dining hall to eat.

She shoved the rest of the cannoli in her mouth, wiped her hands together and sprinted the rest of the way to Nans.

The four ladies turned as Lexy tapped lightly on the screen then let herself in. She glanced at the white board and noticed they had added a column labeled 'clues' and put 'pink Cadillac' under it and had updated the 'Dugasse' column with the time of death.

"Did Payne say anything enlightening after we left?" Nans was all business.

"Not really." Lexy sunk into the old slip covered sofa that faced the white board and studied the columns.

"Let's go through the board and you can tell us about any new information," Nans said to Lexy.

"Did you find out about any enemies or any rumors about Chef Dugasse?"

Lexy shook her head. "Nothing so far. I have Deena asking around. You know how teens are, they see a lot more than the rest of us."

Nans nodded, then pointed to the 'Crime Scene' column. "Do you know what they might have found for evidence?"

"Other than the knife? No. But Jack said, if it was his case, he would be scouring the trails for evidence and it doesn't look like Payne is doing that. We walked a couple of them yesterday and didn't find a thing, but there's one more I want to check out ... maybe you guys could go with me?"

"Sure," Nans said, looking at the others who nodded their agreement.

"I wish we knew if they found anything out by the dumpsters," Helen said. "It sure is a lot easier investigating these things when you have an 'in' at the police department."

Lexy nodded her agreement. Back home, Jack usually knew everything about the cases they were working on and he would give them tidbits of information. She didn't think they'd be getting the same courtesy from Payne.

Nans pointed at the murder weapon column on the white board. "This knife could be a clue … if we could verify whose knife it is."

Lexy shrugged. "Most every chef has a set of knives, but I did notice that knife was a very high end one with a mahogany handle. I haven't seen any like that in the kitchen but I'll keep looking."

Ida stepped out from the other side of the board and tapped her finger on the heading of the next column, 'Sylvia'. "This is probably where we should focus our efforts."

"Yes, she seems to be our most likely suspect," Nans agreed.

"She claims she was in the freezer, that she never went outside until after I found him," Lexy said. "Thomas, the chef she was talking to right before the murder said he didn't see where she went, so I can't place her at the scene … yet."

"She stands to gain the head chef spot and she probably hated him just as much as anyone," Helen pointed out.

"I bet when she saw him yelling at the other chef, it was the straw that broke the camel's back and she got so mad that she ran out there and shoved the knife into his chest!" Ida clasped her hands together and arced them in the air in front of her, making stabbing motions.

Ruth nodded. "Pent up aggression for how he treated everyone."

"A crime of passion," Helen added.

Helen's words triggered something in the back of Lexy's mind. "Or maybe ..."

The four women raised their eyebrows at her.

"What if there was more going on with Sylvia and Dugasse than just a chef and sous-chef relationship?" Lexy asked.

Nans eyebrows shot up. "Did you see something to indicate that?"

"Well, sort of. I did see them in some conversations that seemed to be more personal then professional. I didn't think anything of it at the time, but now ..."

"A lover's quarrel!" Ida's eyes lit up.

"Well, I don't know. It's one thing to look into, I guess. There's another thing too." Lexy's brow wrinkled. "When Sylvia saw me with the body, she asked if we should hide it."

"Hide it?" Nans said. "Why would she ask that if she didn't kill him?"

"I have no idea," Lexy said. "And then there's the matter of Brad."

"Who's Brad?" Helen asked.

"Another one of the chefs. He's the one that told Payne I had stormed off to 'stop Dugasse once and for all'. *And* he was needling me today about being the killer." Lexy pressed her lips together. "I have no idea why he would do that, unless he just hates me."

"It could be a love triangle!" Ida said.

Lexy made a face. "I'll have to ask around and see if anyone else noticed anything."

"Meanwhile, I'll add Brad to the board." Nans added his name under the 'Suspects' column.

"There's another thing to consider," Ruth said. "How did his body get *behind* the dumpster?"

"He might have been dragged there to buy some time for the killer. If the feet weren't sticking out he might not have been found until hours later." Nans pinched her nose with her thumb and forefinger. "The smell of the dumpster would have masked any smells from the body."

"And that would imply the killer wanted to get far away ... so maybe it wasn't someone from the kitchen," Helen said.

"Or, he was lured to the other side of the dumpster by the killer, who stabbed him, then took off down the path," Ida added.

"Either way, that indicates we should also consider suspects that weren't in the kitchen," Nans said.

"Which ties in with what I found online." Ruth held up the iPad.

Lexy's eyebrows shot up. "What did you find?"

"Well, it seems your chef was involved in some sort of chili contest," Ruth said.

Lexy nodded remembering Brad's order that she make the cornbread was the catalyst for her finding Dugasse in the first place. "Yes, I know."

"Well, it seems this chili contest can be quite lucrative and it's very competitive ... some newspaper articles describe it as 'cutthroat.'"

"Why?" Helen asked.

"The usual reason. Money. The winner gets a national brand so not only will they get the money from chili sales, but their name will become a household word which will lead to other endorsements, cookbooks etc. ..." Ruth looked up at them. "Winning that contest could be worth millions."

"Did he ever talk about the contest? His rivals, or anything?" Nans asked Lexy.

"I never heard him say anything." Lexy spread her hands wishing she'd paid more attention to Dugasse, the truth was she kind of zoned out whenever he started droning on.

"Well, that's something to look into then." Ruth crossed to the board and added 'Chili Contest' to the list.

"And that brings us to the pink Cadillac." Helen pointed to the words on the white board.

"Too bad we can't ask Jack to just look that up in the database," Ida said.

"Well, luckily a pink Cadillac is unusual, so I'm going to start by doing a search on newspaper articles. Then if that doesn't pan out, I'll hack into the motor vehicles database." Ruth looked up at them and widened her eyes, putting her hand over her mouth. "Ooops ... I mean I'll look elsewhere."

The other women laughed, then gathered behind Ruth to look over her shoulder as she searched.

After a minute she said, "Got it!"

She held the iPad up. "Here's a picture of the exact same car I saw in the parking lot. The article is about a semi-celebrity that's staying in the area at the Sheraton Hotel. You know the fancy five star one, on the side of the mountain?"

"Yes," Nans, Ida, Helen and Lexy all said. Everyone knew that hotel. It was the height of luxury.

"Well, apparently she loves pink. Pink car. Pink clothes. Pink purse. Even a pink dog."

Lexy wrinkled her brow and bent closer to the iPad. Sure enough, it showed a middle-aged blonde with gigantic pink sunglasses holding a furry dyed-pink Pomeranian.

"What's that have to do with our case?" Nans wondered.

Lexy grabbed the iPad and scanned the article. Her heart jerked in her chest when she looked at the caption under the picture. She sucked in a deep breath and looked up at the four women.

"The owner of the pink Cadillac is Victoria Dugasse ... Chef Dugasse's wife."

Chapter Eight

"Thanks for making the cake, Lexy," Nans said as she slid into the backseat of Ruth's gigantic Oldsmobile beside Lexy.

Lexy looked down at the red velvet cake on the seat beside her. She'd had to cut her beach time with Jack short to make it yesterday afternoon and he'd been unusually understanding. In fact, he seemed strangely disinterested in the case and the fact that she was a murder suspect.

"Lexy?"

"Oh sorry, I was just thinking how Jack seems only interested in fishing, he didn't even care that we were going to visit Victoria Dugasse today. Normally he'd have all kinds of warnings about butting into police stuff."

Ida turned in the front seat to face her.

"Oh, that's how they get. When it comes to fishing they become obsessed. I know Norman is. He has only fishing on his mind ... well that and one other thing." Ida winked at Lexy who shifted uncomfortably in her seat, unwanted pictures of Ida and Norman bubbling up in her mind.

Ruth maneuvered the car out of the resort and headed up the highway. Lexy wondered how she managed—her eyes barely cleared the top of the steering wheel. Lexy tested her seatbelt to make sure it was fastened properly.

"Do you really think she'll buy our ruse of wanting to give our condolences?" Helen asked.

"I don't see why not. It's the proper thing to do," Nans replied. "Besides, we'll make it seem like we are on official business from the resort, then she'll be more likely to talk to us."

"Hopefully we can get her to open up enough to tell us where she was that morning," Ida said. "Because if she wasn't in the kitchen ..."

"... She could have been out by the dumpster with Dugasse." Nans finished the sentence.

"Well I doubt she's going to tell us she killed him." Lexy cringed as Ruth turned into the parking lot for the hotel, her back tires going up over the curb and crushing a bed of petunias.

"No, but hopefully we'll be able to tell if she's hiding something," Nans said as Ruth parked the car.

Everyone got out. Lexy grabbed the cake and followed the four women into the gigantic hotel, happy to have gotten there in one piece.

The lobby was sumptuous. Lexy's sandals sunk into thick carpeting in a dark blue and gold pattern as she walked past the giant marble table that held a vase of flowers which must have been six feet tall and three feet wide. A crystal chandelier sparkled above the flowers.

Nans walked past the oak paneled front desk and straight to the elevators. Ruth had somehow gotten the room number so they knew just where to go. They rode the elevator up to the eighth floor, turned left and walked the fifty feet to room 845.

Nans knocked on the door. Lexy heard the safety chain slide, then the door opened a crack. A baby blue eye peeked out at them.

"Yes?"

"Mrs. Dugasse?" Nans asked.

"Yes." The door swung open to reveal a tall blonde who raised her perfectly plucked eyebrows at them. Lexy noticed she was wearing an expensive pink silk sleeveless shirt and white capri-length pants. Her bare feet sported petal pink painted toenails and gigantic pink diamonds glittered in her ears.

"We're from Lakeshore Resort. We'd like to express our condolences," Nans said as Lexy shoved the cake in Victoria's face.

"Oh. Do come in." The door swung open and they stepped inside while introducing themselves.

"Please call me Victoria," their host said as she took the cake from Lexy. "Would you like a piece?"

"No thanks," Nans said and the rest of them shook their heads.

Victoria put the cake on a sideboard and gestured them further into the opulent suite. They settled in the living room—Victoria, Nans and Ida picked out chairs while Ruth, Helen and Lexy shared the sofa. The room was decorated with French provincial furniture in off white. Pink curtains and throw pillows accented the white upholstered sofa and chairs. Lexy wondered if the hotel just happened to have a pink room or if Victoria had redecorated.

A white Pomeranian with pink tipped fur pitter patted into the room.

"You dyed your dog's fur?" Lexy asked.

"Yes, well, just the ends." Victoria picked the tiny pooch up—a girl Lexy assumed by the pink bow—kissed the top of her head, then set the dog on her lap. "My hairdresser says it is quite safe."

A motion to Lexy's left caught her attention. She turned her head and felt her eyebrows shoot up. It was a maid, in a black and white uniform. Who has a maid in a hotel room?

"Oh Myra, why don't you bring us some lemonade." Victoria glanced at Nans and the rest of them who nodded. "Six lemonades, then."

Myra disappeared and Nans put her hand on Victoria's arm. "We're so sorry about the loss of your husband."

"Thank you." Victoria dabbed at her eyes with a tissue even though there were no tears. Lexy noticed that pink and white diamond rings were stacked on almost all of her fingers. Her wrist displayed a flashy Rolex watch.

"You knew Alain?" She asked after the appropriate amount of eye dabbing.

Nans nodded. "We enjoyed his food. Lexy here is the pastry chef in the kitchen at the resort."

"Chef Dugasse will be missed," Lexy said forcing a smile at Victoria, then crossing her fingers behind her back and hoping not to get struck by lightning.

The maid came in saving Lexy from having to say anything more. She handed out crystal glasses filled with lemonade—pink lemonade, of course.

With the formalities dispensed, Nans got right to the point. "You were there that morning, right?"

Victoria's eyes went wide. "Well ... I ..."

"I noticed your lovely pink car," Ruth said. "It's quite distinctive ... hard to miss."

"Oh, yes. I suppose I was there. Earlier." Victoria took a sip of lemonade.

"To see your husband?" Nans asked.

"Yes."

"And you had a fight." Nans persisted.

Victoria's eyebrows mashed together. "How did you know that?"

"Oh, one hears things ..." Nans waved her hands. "It must be very disturbing to you to have been fighting right before he ... well, you know."

"Yes, it is very sad for my last memory to be of that fight. Although I doubt Alain would feel the same way."

Nans looked at Victoria over the rim of her lemonade glass. "Why do you say that?"

"Because, Alain was having an affair."

***

Nans eyebrows shot up. "An affair? What makes you say that?"

Victoria shrugged. "He had been sneaking off at around two in the morning on several nights. He thought I didn't notice that he got up early and left."

"And you confronted him about that?" Ida asked.

"Yes, of course. I used it as leverage to stop him from curtailing my spending." Victoria waved her hand around the room. "I need to be kept in the manner to which I've become accustomed."

"What did he say when you confronted him?" Lexy asked.

"He denied having the affair. Typical cheater." Victoria studied her frosty pink nails. Lexy noticed that she didn't seem very upset about the affair or his death.

"Do you have any idea *who* he was having the affair with?"

"Nope. It could have been anyone," Victoria said.

"So, you were using the knowledge of the affair as leverage to keep your spending habits, but why? How would that help you?"

"It's all in the prenup. Alain would lose a lot of money if he had an affair."

Lexy saw Nans exchange glances with Ida, Ruth and Helen.

"But, if you killed him, then you'd get to keep all the money either way," Nans said.

Victoria's back stiffened.

"Is that what you think? That *I* killed him?" She dumped the pink pooch on the floor and shot out of her chair. Storming over to the door, she held it open gesturing for them to leave.

Lexy took the hint and got up from her chair as did Nans, Ruth, Ida and Helen. They filed out the door.

Victoria stood in the doorway and watched them go.

"And for your information," she yelled after them, "I didn't need, or want to kill him. The truth is Alain would have made even more money after he won the *Chili Battle*. So, you see, he was worth much more to me alive than dead."

***

"She didn't seem too upset about her husband being dead," Lexy said once they were strapped into Ruth's Oldsmobile and heading back to the resort.

"But she sure got upset when she thought we were accusing her of killing him," Ida added.

"That doesn't necessarily mean she killed him." Ruth looked at Lexy in the rear view mirror.

"I doubt she is the killer," Nans said. "If Dugasse was going to become even richer because of winning the *Chili Battle*, it wouldn't be in her best interest to kill him."

"Unless he was going to divorce her and leave her out in the cold," Ida ventured. "Maybe that's what they argued about."

Lexy pressed her lips together. "I wonder who he was sneaking off to see in the early morning. That seems like an odd time to meet a secret lover."

"I bet it was that Sylvia Spicer. They had a lover's spat and she killed him," Ruth said.

Lexy blew out a whoosh of air. "Maybe. There's a lot of things we still need to look into. Like where that other trail leads and if Sylvia really *was* in the freezer when Dugasse was being stabbed. *And* we need to find out more about this chili contest. How come everyone is so certain that Dugasse was going to win?"

"Good question," Nans said. "We do have our work cut out for us."

Ruth rolled down her window and stuck her hand out to signal for the turn.

"Ruth, you know that most everyone uses the directionals on the steering column now, right?" Ida turned around and rolled her eyes at Nans, Helen and Lexy in the back seat.

Ruth ignored her and made the turn, almost clipping the outer corner of the sign for the resort.

"Do you want me to drop you off at your cottage, Lexy?" Ruth asked.

Lexy glanced at her watch. "Actually, why don't you drop me off at the dining lodge? I have to make tarts today, but I'm going to do a bit of poking around first ... to see if I can get any of these questions answered."

Chapter Nine

Ruth dropped Lexy off at the main entrance to the dining hall. The dining room was empty at this time of day and Lexy skirted her way down the cedar log wall, in between the rustic tables, and past the giant window that had a panoramic view of the lake. She turned left at the two story stone fireplace, then ducked into an obscure hallway that led to the restaurant offices.

Lexy stopped at a large office. Prescott Charles, the restaurant manager, was sitting at his desk in a crisp white short sleeved shirt and light blue tie. Lexy tapped softly on the door.

Prescott looked up from the paperwork he had been studying. "Hi, Lexy. Come on in."

He half stood indicating for Lexy to sit in a faux leather chair across from his desk. Lexy noticed a musky scent lingering in the air as she entered the room. It niggled something in her memory, but she didn't have time to dig deep enough to figure out what it was.

"So, what can I do for you?" Prescott steepled his fingers together, his light green eyes questioning her from behind his mahogany desk. Behind him, Lexy noticed a wall of bookshelves filled with various books on subjects ranging from restaurant management to log cabin building to decorating. Family photos of Prescott with his wife and kids dotted the shelves.

Lexy shifted in her chair, suddenly thinking maybe this wasn't such a great idea. Prescott raised his brows.

"Um ... Well, I was wondering if there's any type of surveillance in the kitchen. You know cameras that record what's going on," Lexy said.

"Surveillance? Why would you want to know about that?"

"Well, umm ... Detective Payne seems to think I'm his best suspect for Dugasse's murder and I was thinking the cameras would prove I was in the kitchen when it happened," Lexy lied. She didn't want to tell him the real reason was that she wanted to know if Sylvia Spicer really *was* in the freezer like she claimed. She didn't want to cast any aspersions on Sylvia if she was innocent.

"We don't have anything like that in the kitchen," Prescott said, avoiding eye contact with her.

"Oh, okay." Lexy got up to leave, then turned at the door. "You didn't happen to notice anything strange going on with Sylvia Spicer and Chef Dugasse, did you?"

Prescott jerked in his chair. His elbow hit a cup full of pens and they spilled out on to the floor. He bent down to pick them up and Lexy walked back to the desk and squatted down to help.

Prescott looked at her from under the desk. "Why do you ask that? I didn't notice anything." His voice was choppy, nervous.

"Well, it's probably nothing, but she said something kind of funny to me when we were out at the dumpster after I found Dugasse." Lexy handed him the pens she'd gathered and they both stood up.

"What was that?" Prescott wrinkled his brows at her.

"She asked if we should hide the body."

Prescott sucked in a breath, his eyes going wide, the pencil holder clattering to the floor, pens spilling out all over again.

"What?" He stared at Lexy, his face growing red. He reached up to loosen his tie.

Lexy had a momentary pang of guilt. She felt bad talking about Sylvia ... but it was true and asking around might be the only way to find out what really happened.

"She was probably just so distraught ..." Lexy bent down to help with the pens again but Prescott waved her off.

"I can pick these up." His eyes slid to the door inviting her to leave. "Please close the door behind you."

"Okay, well ... thanks," Lexy said, not sure what she was thanking him for.

She backed out of the office, closing the door quietly behind her. She stood there for a minute, thinking about Prescott's reaction. *Why had he been so nervous when she asked about Sylvia and Dugasse?*

A faint rustle in the hallway behind her and the scent of musk caught her attention. She whirled around. The hallway was empty, but she had turned just in time to see the doorway to the first office slowly closing.

She crept over to the door which was open just a crack. Someone was standing just behind it. Hiding. Lexy reached out, grabbed the knob and wrenched the door open, her heart jerking wildly in her chest as she looked up into the face of Sylvia Spicer.

*****

Sylvia stood in front of her, eyes wide, mouth forming a surprised "Oh." She held something behind her back. A chef's knife? Images of herself as the next victim flashed through Lexy's mind and she took a step backward into the hall.

"What are *you* doing here?" Lexy asked.

"What are you?" Sylvia's eyes darted around the room and out into the hall.

"I came to ask Prescott about ... something." Lexy leaned to the left to get a view of what Sylvia had behind her back.

Sylvia whipped her hand out from behind her back in one fluid motion and Lexy's heart jumped into her throat.

"I came to drop off this invoice," she said, indicating the piece of paper she'd been holding behind her back.

Lexy's shoulders relaxed and she leaned against the doorjamb. Sylvia shot nervous glances at Prescott's door.

"Hey Sylvia, I was wondering something," Lexy said.

"What?"

"When we were out by the dumpster, you said something about hiding Dugasse's body. Why would you say that?"

Sylvia's eyes jerked over to Prescott's door again before she louvered them back at Lexy.

"I did? I must have been so distraught that I didn't know what I was saying." Sylvia shrugged. "Why would I want you to hide the body?"

"That's what I was wondering," Lexy said, then she narrowed her eyes at Sylvia. "Did you get the head chef job ... to replace Dugasse?"

"Yes. Prescott ... I mean, Mr. Charles promoted me to head chef."

"Congratulations. So it looks like Dugasse's death was good for you in that respect. But I bet you miss him."

Sylvia wrinkled her brow and Lexy leaned in closer, lowering her voice. "I heard you were very close with someone here."

Sylvia's face turned red and her eyes did more darting around. "I don't know what you are talking about."

"Well, you know sometimes men in a position of power can be very attractive ... even if they *are* married." Lexy gave Sylvia her best 'you can confide in me' look.

Sylvia's eyes grew wide. "What did you ..."

"Well, sometimes things go wrong and people get hurt. And that might cause the wounded party to do something they wouldn't normally do ... you know out of passion."

Sylvia glared at her. "Are you implying *I* killed Chef Dugasse because I was mad at him?"

"Oh no, I'm just saying bad things can happen sometimes when you get involved." Lexy's heart leapt into her throat when she saw the menacing look on Sylvia's face.

"I don't know what you're talking about but I do know that Dugasse got what he deserved ... it just wasn't at my hands." Sylvia spat out the words, then brushed past Lexy and stormed off down the hall in the opposite direction of Prescott Charles' office, the invoice apparently forgotten.

Lexy stared after her wondering what she meant by 'Dugasse got what he deserved'. *Was Dugasse involved in something that got him killed?*

Lexy stood in the hall, her lips pursed going over her exchange with Sylvia when she thought she saw a shadow moving under the door to Chef Dugasse's office.

Who would be in there?

She crept down the hall. The door was open just slightly and she craned her neck, her heartbeat picking up speed at what she saw inside. Brad Meltzer had one of the desk drawers open and was rummaging through it.

Lexy held her breath. She stood off to one side and prayed Brad wouldn't look over and see her. She watched as he pawed through the drawer, then moved on to the next drawer, then the next and finally started leafing through cookbooks that were stacked on the desk.

What was he doing?

Lexy stepped closer to the door and pushed it open. Brad jumped away from the desk, jerking his head in her direction. His eyes narrowed when he saw Lexy standing there.

"Looking for something?" Lexy asked.

She saw a ripple of anxiety cross Brad's face, then he composed himself and looked down at the desk.

"I needed the schedule ... chef made it out on Monday." Brad picked up the sheet of paper that had been lying in plain sight on the desk and then started out of the room brushing past Lexy who was standing in the doorway, arms crossed against her chest. She stared after him as he went off down the hallway toward the kitchen.

Looking back into the room, she felt an icy chill run up her spine. All of Dugasse's notes and personal effects were in here and, in light of the fact that he had been murdered, she didn't think anyone was supposed to be in his office ... much less rummaging around in the drawers. The schedule was important, but it had been sitting on the top of the desk, surely Brad didn't need to rummage around to find it.

Which begged the question ... what exactly *was* Brad looking for?

Chapter Ten

Deena had the day off, and Lexy was able to whip up the tarts for that evening's dessert at record speed since she didn't have to take time out for giving instructions. Once finished, she threw her apron in the laundry basket and headed off for some well-deserved beach time.

At her cottage, she changed into a white and blue striped one piece and threw on a long sleeved white shirt as a cover-up. Tossing Sprinkles a treat, she shoved a towel in her oversized beach bag and headed down to the small beach at the end of her street.

The beach was dotted with colorful blankets and beach umbrellas. Kids played at making sand castles, parents sat in beach chairs next to coolers and teens ran through the water laughing and diving.

Lexy spotted Jack lying on a lounge chair about ten feet from the edge of the water. She slipped off her flip flops to feel the warm, course sand on her feet and started toward him.

"Hi handsome, is this spot taken?" Lexy spread her towel down beside Jack who peered over the top of his book at her.

"I suppose you can sit here, but only until my wife comes down."

Lexy laughed, then bent over to kiss him before plopping down on the towel.

"So how was your visit with the widow?" Jack asked.

"Interesting." Lexy dug in her beach bag for suntan lotion. "She said Dugasse was worth more to her alive than dead."

Jack raised an eyebrow. "How so?"

"Well, he was a shoo-in to win that *Chili Battle*. You know, the one they are having here at the fairgrounds." Lexy pointed in the direction of the open field in the middle of the resort. "Anyway, I guess winning that means you get a lot of money thrown at you."

"Hmmm." Jack pursed his lips.

"Oh, and she also said that she thought Dugasse was having an affair because he snuck out in the wee hours of the morning."

"But she was there the morning he was killed, right?" Jack asked.

"Yes, but she said she didn't kill him."

"They all say that." Jack dog-eared a page and then closed his book. "But she might have a point about him being worth more money. Does she have an alibi?"

Lexy's brows mashed together. She dumped out the contents of her bag, still unable to find the suntan lotion. "I don't know. She didn't seem very hospitable after Nans practically accused her of killing Dugasse, so we got out of there fast."

Jack laughed. "Well, maybe you could check the hotel. Or maybe Payne has already done that. The room keys record when people come and go so if she was back in her room at the time of death, it would show that."

"Well, I don't think Payne is going to share any of that information with me. He's not as nice as you are with that sort of stuff." Lexy grabbed the copper colored bottle of sun tan lotion and opened the top. Squirting some on her arm, she started rubbing it in. "But I don't think the wife is the killer."

"Oh, why not?"

"I ran into Sylvia Spicer when I was at the dining lodge and she was acting really funny. Nans and the ladies were thinking she might be the one Dugasse was having an affair with, so I kind of hinted around about that and she got really mad."

Jack chuckled. "Well, wouldn't you, if someone was hinting around that you had an affair and murdered someone?"

"Yeah, probably." Lexy pressed her lips together. Maybe Sylvia *was* only reacting to her accusations. "But I found out some other strange things today too."

"What?" Jack took the bottle from her and started rubbing lotion on her legs, venturing into parts that were already covered by her suit and causing her to almost forget what she was saying.

"What? Oh ... when I was at the dining hall I talked to Prescott Charles, the manager, and he was acting kind of strange about the whole Dugasse thing and then I caught Brad Meltzer sneaking around in Dugasse's office!"

Jack finished with the lotion and looked at her. "Well, it sounds like you have a lot of things to follow up on before you can get a picture of what is really going on."

"Right." Lexy bit her bottom lip. There *was* a lot to figure out ... could she, Nans and the *Ladies Detective Club* handle all that?

"You know what I'd do?" Jack prompted.

"What?"

"I'd start with one clue and follow it through to the end. Knock off each of your questions one by one until they are all resolved and then you'll know the truth."

"You make it sound so easy." Lexy opened her bag and started putting the contents that she had spilled on her towel back inside it.

"It's not that hard if you take it one at a time," Jack said. "Did you ever get back to that other trail?"

"No, I was planning on doing that later today. Wanna come?"

"I wish I could, but I'm going fishing." Jack peered over his sunglasses at her. "You're not going alone, I hope."

"Oh no, Nans and the ladies will be with me so I'll be perfectly safe."

"That's great. I'm *sure* you won't get into any trouble with them," Jack said dubiously as he pushed his sunglasses up on his face and flipped over on his stomach.

Lexy leaned back on her elbows and watched the lake lap at the shore. A little bird ran along the edge of the water pecking for food. Out on the lake, people paddled on kayaks and canoes. The occasional motor boat sped by in the deeper waters. It was calm. Relaxing.

Lexy's stomach twisted to think a murderer could be running loose right in this very resort. And, since Payne didn't seem to be doing a very good job, it might be up to Lexy and the *Ladies Detective Club* to catch the killer.

Chapter Eleven

Lexy had just finished showering and was wrestling Sprinkles into her harness when Nans, Ruth and Helen appeared at her cottage door.

"Where's Ida?" Lexy asked.

"Oh she begged off," Nans said.

"Claimed she had to do something with Norman before he went out fishing tonight." Ruth giggled.

Lexy made a face and held her hand up. Considering Ida's comment earlier that day about the two things fishermen were interested in, she didn't want to know anymore.

"Will you guys be okay? This could be a long walk and a lot of it is uphill." Lexy realized the three women were clutching their giant patent leather old ladies purses. "You're not bringing those purses, are you?"

"We bring these everywhere," Helen said.

"They're loaded up with all kinds of useful items," Ruth added.

"You never know when something in here is going to come in handy." Nans opened her purse and angled it toward Lexy.

"They look heavy," Lexy said. "Why don't you leave them here and you can pick them up on the way back? You'll be able to walk the path easier without them."

The three women looked at each other. Nans held her purse out by the handles as if judging the weight, then nodded.

"You may be right, dear," she said and put her purse on the table. Ruth and Helen did the same with theirs.

"Okay, let's get this show on the road." Nans opened the door, leading the way outside.

They followed the same path Lexy and Jack and followed the other day. When they got to the top of the hill, Lexy had to stop to catch her breath.

"You guys don't even seem winded." She stared at Nans, Ruth and Helen.

"Oh, that's nothing," Nans said. "We do yoga, Pilates and water aerobics ... a little hill like this is child's play."

"Maybe you should consider joining us in our regular workout." Ruth frowned at Lexy. "You seem a bit out of shape.

Lexy looked down at her slim body. *Out of shape?* Well, sure she was a bit winded after the climb but she still *looked* good. At least that's what Jack had said down at the beach.

"You're not in your twenties anymore," Nans added looking her up and down. "And you won't be able to keep that cute shape without having to work at it for long."

"Yeah, you don't think our girlish figures come without a price, do you?" Helen ran her hands up and down the sides of her body and everyone laughed.

"Okay, where's this path?" Nans asked.

"Over here." Lexy pulled Sprinkles to the end of the path and walked the short distance to the back of the dining hall where the trails intersected.

Nans glanced over at the dumpster, still marked with crime scene tape. "Is that where ...?"

"Yep, that's where I found him." Lexy shivered despite the warm afternoon air.

Ruth walked right up to the crime scene tape. "Maybe we should take a little look around. The police may have overlooked a clue."

"Good idea," Helen said. She held the tape up while Nans and Ruth scooted under, then ducked under it herself.

The smell of old fish, sour milk and rotting cabbage assaulted Lexy and she pinched her nose shut.

"Can you guys hurry up?" she said, except it came out as 'hubby up'.

Nans bent down, scuffing at the debris under the dumpster with her shoe. "Come take a look at this."

Ruth and Helen bent over to take a look. Lexy pinched her nose even tighter and got as close as she dared, craning over the crime scene tape to see what they had found.

"Is that ...?" Ruth asked.

"I do believe it is," Helen replied.

Nans worked at something with her shoe, sliding it out from under the dumpster. She pulled a kleenex out of her pocket, then bent over to pick up the item. She stood holding it in the air, careful to touch it only with the kleenex.

"Is that blood?" Lexy asked. The item Nans held up looked to be a swatch of fabric—plaid flannel. It was about one inch square and a rust colored smear on it that looked suspiciously like blood. *But, whose blood?*

"I think so," Nans said. Wrapping the fabric in the tissue, she slid it into her pocket.

"Is that Dugasse's blood?" Ruth asked.

"It could be. But the fabric was wedged under the dumpster so it could have been there before he was murdered."

"Or it could have come from the killer."

"I wish we had our own forensics lab." Nans pressed her lips together. "I don't trust that Detective Payne not to fumble this up. He didn't even find that fabric when he searched the area!"

"True. He seems like a dope," Ruth said.

"I don't see anything else. Do either of you?" Helen asked.

"Nope. Let's move on," Ruth answered and the three of them scurried under the crime scene tape and then joined Lexy at the intersection of the paths.

"So which path?" Nans looked at Lexy.

"Well, this one goes to the front parking lot so I doubt the killer used that one," Lexy said pointing to the path on the left. Then she turned and pointed to one of the middle paths. "And this is the only other one I haven't walked on."

"Well, let's go!" Ruth started in the direction of the path in a power walk and Lexy trotted after her.

"We should slow down and look for clues ... you know anything unusual," Lexy said remembering Jack's advice.

"Yes, we know what clues are, dear," Nans teased.

They walked leisurely letting Sprinkles make her various pit stops. They were only about twenty feet down the path when Sprinkles found something she must have thought was irresistible. Lexy tugged on the leash, but Sprinkles insisted on sniffing whatever it was she had found under a small shrub.

"What have you got, Sprinks?" Lexy bent down to investigate hoping it wasn't a dead animal. It wasn't. Lexy picked it up and held it out for the ladies.

"What is it?" Nans narrowed her eyes at the thin strip of leather with stainless steel spikes sticking out of it.

"I think it's a bracelet," Ruth said.

Lexy wrapped it around her wrist and it snapped closed with magnetic clasps on each end. Ruth was right. "Who would wear a bracelet like this?" Lexy asked.

"Maybe one of the teenagers?" Nans said. "Their ever changing fashions always baffle me."

"Maybe." Lexy put the bracelet in her pocket and started forward. "I'll just keep it ... it could be a clue."

The ladies nodded and followed her down the path. Like the previous day, the tall trees provided welcome shade. The birds chirped, chipmunks scurried in the leaves and the smell of the woods made the walk relaxing and pleasant. Until they came to a section that became very dense ... and dark.

Lexy hesitated, looking at the others. "Is it getting dark out?"

"No, it's just the woods are really thick here." Nans looked back behind them. "The trail narrows, but it keeps going."

Nans forged ahead and Lexy followed. They had to walk single file since the trail was so thin and dense forest on either side made it impossible to stray. They walked in silence, Lexy's nerves getting more jittery with every step.

Nans stopped abruptly and Lexy almost rammed into her.

"There's a clearing up ahead." Nans pointed. Lexy craned around her to see. It looked like the path ended in a clearing with a small camp in the middle.

"Let's check it out," Helen whispered.

They scuffled up to the end of the path where they could get a better view of the small house. A picnic table sat in between the path and the camp and there was a large campfire pit in front of it. Six motorcycles were lined up next to the house. No one seemed to be there except a large Boxer dog that lay snoring on the porch.

Nans motioned for them to crouch down behind a bush and they all obeyed.

"I wonder who stays here?" She whispered.

Lexy shrugged. "Do you think they take the path to the dining hall?"

"I don't know. Someone does."

The Boxer lifted its head and started sniffing.

Sprinkles sniffed too and wiggled around. Lexy pulled the dog tight beside her. "Shhh.."

Lexy's heartbeat kicked up a notch when she saw the Boxer get up from his place on the porch. He lifted his nose in the air, sniffed, then turned in their direction.

Sprinkles started to growl.

The Boxer started walking toward them.

Lexy shushed Sprinkles again.

The Boxer came even closer and Sprinkles let out a yelp, then darted out from behind the bush, yanking the leash out of Lexy's hand and running in the direction of the Boxer.

Lexy jumped up, her heart jerking in her chest.

"Sprinkles come back!" She started off toward the dogs ready to grab Sprinkles from the clutches of the menacing Boxer. Sprinkles stopped in front of the Boxer and the two dogs calmly started sniffing each other.

Lexy felt her shoulders relax, then the door of the cabin exploded open and two burly guys in leather vests burst out. One of them had a shotgun and the other a knife.

Lexy's heart pounded against her ribcage as the largest guy—the one with the bandana on his bald head and spider tattoo on his neck—pointed the shotgun at her.

"Who are you?" he demanded.

Lexy's mouth went dry. She tried to swallow but it was like drinking sandpaper.

"I told you we should have brought our purses." She heard Nans whisper from behind the shrub.

The big guy narrowed his eyes in the direction of the shrub. "Who's that? Is someone behind that bush?"

Lexy looked back over her shoulder and her heart sank as she saw Nans, Ruth and Helen all stand up, their hands held up next to their heads, palms out.

"We're just some little old ladies from the resort." Nans nodded at Lexy and Sprinkles. "I was just taking my granddaughter and her dog for a walk."

The two guys cut their eyes to the dogs who had gotten around to sniffing each other's back ends. Lexy thought the dogs seemed to be making friends a lot easier than their owners.

"Hey, looks like Brutus found a friend," the smaller guy said.

The big guy narrowed his eyes at the dog, lowering the gun slightly then jerked it back up in Lexy's direction. "Who sent you?"

Lexy's brows mashed together. "Sent me? No one."

The two guys exchanged a glance. The smaller guy put his knife away and shrugged.

"They're grandmas," he said pointing his chin in Nans direction.

The big guy nodded, but kept his gun trained on Lexy. "I suggest you take your dog, get on out of here and don't come back."

Lexy ran over and grabbed Sprinkles leash. "Right. No problem. Sorry."

She turned and sprinted back toward the path, making sure Nans, Ruth and Helen got away ahead of her.

She glanced back over her shoulder every twenty steps and her heart didn't stop racing until they were a full five minutes away.

"What was that all about?" Nans asked.

"I'm not sure but it seemed like a gang of unfriendly bikers to me," Ruth answered.

"Do you think they could have had something to do with Chef Dugasse's murder?" Helen asked.

"I bet they either had something to do with it, or they know something," Lexy said.

"Just because they are bikers and acted like they didn't want us in their camp is no reason to assume they are killers," Nans admonished.

"It's not just that." Lexy pulled the bracelet she'd found at the head of the trail out of her pocket and held it up in front of her. "The guy with the knife had this exact same bracelet on and, since this one was found only twenty feet from the dining hall, I think it's safe to assume one of them has been to that kitchen at least once before."

Chapter Twelve

Lexy dipped her spoon into the thick custard and brought it to her lips. The sweetness from the sugar and the unmistakable flavor from the real vanilla bean she'd added danced on her tongue. The creaminess of the custard was like velvet in her mouth. Perfect.

She pulled over a tray of the small puff pastries she'd made to house the custard and set the bowl of chocolate she'd drizzle on the top next to her. Spooning the custard into a piping bag, she picked up a pastry, squeezed some custard inside then set it on another tray. She continued until she had one tray completed, then spooned the chocolate on top for a perfect set of miniature bite-sized éclairs.

She popped one into her mouth letting the flavorful explosion thrill her taste buds. They were just the way she wanted. She pulled another tray of puff pastries over and started repeating the process.

As she filled the pastries she thought about the previous evening's excursion with Nans and the ladies. Could the biker gang have something to do with Dugasse's murder? Why would

Dugasse be involved with them? It didn't make any sense.

She was trying to figure out how she could find out more about the bikers and what they were doing there when a grating voice cut into her thoughts from across the room.

"Miss Baker, what a surprise to find you here in the kitchen instead of pestering suspects."

Lexy's stomach tightened as she watched Detective Payne make his way over to her. He wore his usual plaid Bermuda shorts and had his spiral bound notebook and pencil in hand. His eyes slid from hers to the tray of éclairs.

"I have no idea what you mean," Lexy said feigning innocence.

"You went to visit Victoria Dugasse?" He raised an eyebrow at her.

"My grandmother and I paid our condolences."

"Hmm ... well, she seemed to think you were doing more than that." Grabbing an éclair from the tray, he stuffed it into his mouth before continuing. "I'd appreciate it if you left the police business to the police ... besides the wife didn't to it. The hotel records show that she was in the hotel gym at the time of death."

Lexy's eyebrows shot up. That was one person she could cross off her suspect list. She decided to test out Payne to see how much he knew.

She leaned closer to him and lowered her voice. "So, she didn't kill him because of his affair with Sylvia Spicer?"

Payne's forehead collapsed in a network of wrinkles. "Spicer? What makes you think they were having an affair?"

"They seemed awfully close. In fact Sylvia came right out after I found him and was very upset."

"Well, of course she would be upset. Her boss was dead." Payne glanced around the room looking for Sylvia, no doubt. "Maybe you are just implicating Sylvia because she has the damaging statement of finding you leaning over the dead body."

Lexy pressed her lips together and leaned even closer. "Well, there is the matter of her getting promoted."

Payne nodded. "Yes, yes. We know all about that. We *are* the police you know. But Spicer wasn't having the affair with Dugasse."

"How do you know that? The wife told us he was sneaking off."

Payne waved his hand around dismissively. "Sneaking around does not necessarily mean an affair. Like I said, you should leave the detecting to the detectives. You are, after all, one of the suspects."

Lexy felt irritation spark in her chest. Why did Payne keep defending Sylvia and insisting that Lexy was a suspect? It was becoming clear that she was going to have to dig out the clues herself if she wanted to get her name off his radar.

"So I have your word you will leave this Chef Martino Marchesi alone?"

Lexy's heart skipped. Who was Chef Martino Marchesi?

Payne must have caught her confused look. "Don't try to play dumb. I know that you already know Marchesi is the favorite to win the *Chili Battle*."

"*Chili Battle*?" Lexy's brows mashed together. Did Dugasse's death have something to do with the *Chili Battle*?

Payne flapped his arms in exasperation. "Look Baker, you're still high up on the suspect list, but I'm working to cover all the bases and make sure I get the real killer. If you continue to meddle in this case I will have no choice but to stop you ... even if I have to throw you in jail."

Payne grabbed another éclair, popped it into his mouth and pointed the eraser end of his pencil at her and said, "Consider yourself warned."

Then he turned on his heel and stomped off toward the exit.

***

Lexy finished the éclairs as fast as she could and then ran down to Nans' cottage.

"You guys won't believe it ... I just found another clue!" Lexy burst through the front door of the cottage. Nans, Ida, Ruth and Helen were seated at the table shoveling cheeseburgers onto large plates of salad.

"Would you like a cheeseburger salad?" Nans asked.

Lexy narrowed her eyes at the plates. "No buns? Are you guys back on the Paleo diet?"

Nans waffled her hand over the table. "We're just trying to cut down on the carbs."

"Did you say something about a clue, dear?" Ida speared a piece of lettuce, a tomato and then a chunk of burger and brought it up to her mouth.

"Yes. Payne came to the kitchen to yell at me about visiting Dugasse's wife and he let a clue slip. Something about another chef that was connected with the *Chili Battle* contest."

Nans narrowed her eyes. "I knew the chili contest had to figure in here somewhere. What was the chef's name?"

Lexy pursed her lips together wishing she had written the name down. "It was Italian sounding ... I think it was Martin Parcheesi. Does that ring a bell with anyone?"

The ladies looked around at each other shaking their heads.

"No, but we can Google him." Ruth got up from her chair and went over to the iPad. Lexy watched as her fingers tapped on the screen.

"I don't find any Chef Parcheesi. Let me look up this chili contest."

Nans, Ida and Helen munched away at their salads while Lexy went to look over Ruth's shoulder.

"So, is this Parcheesi guy another suspect? Along with the wife, the sous-chef, and the bikers?" Helen asked.

"Seems like we're really piling them up." Ida cleaned the last of the salad out of her bowl and brought it to the sink.

"Actually, the wife has been cleared. Payne let it slip that she has an alibi for the time of the murder," Lexy said.

"Oh good." Ida walked over to the white board. "I'll cross her off the list then."

"Do you mean Chef Martino Marchesi?" Ruth looked up at Lexy.

"Yes!" Lexy snapped her fingers. "That's it!"

"Well, he is involved with the *Chili Battle*. He's one of the front runners," Ruth said.

"So Payne thinks he might have killed Dugasse to win the contest?" Nans stood up and brought her and Helen's bowls to the sink.

"He just warned me to stay away from him. He didn't say why but he said I should stay away from the suspects, so I assume Marchesi is one." Lexy watched Ida write 'Marchesi' on the whiteboard in the suspect column.

"Seems a little drastic to kill someone to win a contest," Helen said.

"Apparently not if you are this Marchesi guy." Ruth tapped the iPad with her finger. "He has ties to organized crime and there's some articles here that put him in a questionable light."

Nans raised her brows. "Is he here in town now?"

"I'd have to check local hotels," Ruth said.

"Do you think he could have some involvement with those bikers we saw yesterday? Maybe he hired them to do his dirty work or something," Helen offered.

"Maybe." Nans studied the white board. "What about Sylvia? Did you find anything more about her supposed affair with Dugasse?"

"That's another thing Payne said. He seemed sure Sylvia was not the one having the affair with him. But she acted so strangely when I confronted her yesterday," Lexy said.

"Well, I wouldn't necessarily take what Payne says as gospel." Ruth rolled her eyes. "He doesn't seem that competent if you ask me."

Lexy nodded. "You can say that again. I think I might need to have another talk with Sylvia."

"Yes, and we need to figure out if Marchesi was in town when Dugasse was murdered *and* talk to those bikers to find out why the bracelet was near the dining hall," Helen said.

"How are we going to talk to the bikers?" Lexy asked. "They didn't seem very friendly when we were there yesterday."

"Oh, don't worry. I think I have that covered." Nans winked at Lexy. "Meet us here tomorrow at two p.m. and I'll show you how to get even the most adversarial suspect to open up."

Chapter Thirteen

Lexy paced back and forth in her small cottage. Nans and the ladies were at bingo and Jack was out fishing. Which left her with too much alone time on her to think about Dugasse's murder.

Sprinkles lay on the floral cushion that was fitted to the seat of the green wicker rocker. Her eyes followed Lexy as she went back and forth.

"If the killer was this Chef Marchesi, then how come no one saw him in the kitchen?" she asked the little dog.

"Did he hide out by the dumpster and wait for Dugasse to come out? Or maybe he lured him out there?"

She looked at Sprinkles who raised an eyebrow.

"I still think Sylvia Spicer is up to something. She's been acting way to jumpy."

Sprinkles let out a little bark.

"And she asked about hiding the body!"

Sprinkles beat the side of the rocker with her tail.

"Do you have to go out?"

The little white dog jumped off the rocker and ran to the door. Lexy saddled the dog up in her harness and led her out through the porch and into the woods beside the cottage.

It was dusk and the air had cooled considerably. It was a perfect summer night, with peepers peeping and flowers perfuming the air. Lexy looked up and sighed at the perfectly round moon and abundance of bright stars.

Sprinkles rummaged around in the leaves and pine needles and Lexy's thoughts turned to Brad Meltzer rummaging around in Dugasse's desk. Just what *had* he been looking for?

She had to admit, she'd never liked Brad. He always seemed like he was pulling something over on you. But just because he was a pompous jerk didn't mean he was a killer.

Still he *had* tried awfully hard to make her look guilty in front of Payne and he *was* looking for something in Dugasse's office. She didn't fall for that excuse of him looking for the schedule. Surely he would have seen it right on the desk. No, he was up to something, Lexy was sure of it.

She glanced up the hill at the dining hall. At this time of night it would be empty. All the meals had been served and cleared, and the chefs and waitstaff would have gone home.

Maybe *she* should poke around in Dugasse's office herself. If she discovered what Brad had been looking for, that could be a valuable clue—maybe even the clue that cracks the case.

Lexy dragged Sprinkles inside and changed into a pair of black jeans and a black tee-shirt. She tied her hair up in a ponytail, then slipped on a pair of black Keds sneakers. Grabbing a small flashlight, she slipped out her front door and headed up the path to the dining hall.

***

Lexy fingered the key to the kitchen's back door in her pocket.

Should she?

It wasn't too late to turn back. But she did have a key, so it wasn't like she was breaking and entering. Just entering. If anyone asked, she could just say she had to check on some stuff for the next day's desserts.

She slid the key into the lock and clicked the door open.

The kitchen was dark. Lexy didn't want to turn any lights on so she switched on her small flashlight and angled it at the floor.

Her heart thumped loudly in her chest as she made her way down the back passageway that led to Dugasse's office. The passage was more of a storage corridor. It had no windows and was pitch black, but she didn't want to risk going through the dining room with its giant windows to get to the main hallway.

Rounding the corner to the main hall, she found Dugasse's door closed. Her heart squeezed.

What if it was locked?

She reached out for the knob, turned it slowly and then breathed a sigh of relief when it twisted open. She cracked the door and slipped inside, closing the door behind her.

As she approached the desk, she could hear Jack's voice in her head telling her how dangerous it was to come here alone. But he'd also said she should check each clue one by one and this was the perfect time for her to look here. She might not get another chance.

With a shrug, she pushed Jack's nagging voice out of her head, opened a drawer and pointed her flashlight inside. She hunted around in the drawer for a few minutes but found nothing except old papers, pencils and pens.

She moved to the next drawer and came up empty with this one too. Lexy chewed on her bottom lip as she looked around the room. It wasn't surprising that she hadn't find anything in the desk drawers, she'd already seen Brad look in there and he hadn't found what he was looking for.

Maybe she should look somewhere that Brad hadn't already looked?

A filing cabinet in the corner captured her attention. She opened a drawer, slowly so as to not make any noise. Putting the flashlight in her mouth, she leafed through the folders, feeling deflated when all she found was old recipes.

Recipes? Her heart pinged.

Could Brad have been looking for a recipe? *The* recipe. The one for Dugasse's famous chili that everyone thought was going to win him the contest? Maybe Brad had plans to enter the contest on his own with that recipe. Winning the contest would be life changing for a low-level chef like Brad, but was it life-changing enough to kill Dugasse for?

A sudden noise in the hall startled Lexy causing her to drop her flashlight which turned off when it hit the floor.

Who would be here at this time of night?

Lexy's heart hammered against her ribcage as she dropped to her knees and groped for the flashlight. Her hand connected with the cold metal and she clutched the light in her fist.

Then she crouched under the desk and waited.

***

Lexy held her breath expecting someone to burst in the room at any second. She waited several minutes listening to only the sound of her own heartbeat thudding in her ears before she climbed out.

Was someone in the hall?

She crept over to the door and put her ear to it but didn't hear anything. No light came in under the bottom of the door. She cracked the door open slowly and peeked out. Nothing.

Pulling the door the rest of the way open she slipped out into the hall. She was just about to head out the way she had come when a light at the other end of the hall caught her eye. It was coming from under Prescott Charles' door. Someone was in his office!

Lexy tiptoed back down the hall and stood to the side of his door. Shadows moved in the light that spilled out from underneath and she could hear the low murmur of voices. She leaned closer, straining to hear.

"... Killed him ..."

"You ..."

Snatches of conversation drifted out from the office and Lexy pressed even closer. *Were they talking about the murder?*

"... No ... stabbed ..."

Lexy felt her heart jolt ... they *were* talking about the murder. *Who was in there?* She stepped up next to the door, her heart lurching when a floorboard gave her away with a loud groan.

The voices in the room stopped and she froze in her tracks.

"Is someone out there?" She heard a woman say from inside the room.

"No one should be here at this time of night." A man's voice this time, laced with panic.

Lexy's mind whirled. Should she make a run for it, or stay still?

The door jerked open causing her heart to plummet.

Lexy's eyebrows mashed together as her eyes registered the scene in front of her. Sylvia Spicer stood directly on the other side of the door, her beige silk shirt untucked and rumpled. Prescott Charles stood close behind her, his eyes wide, face turning beet red.

"You!" Sylvia pointed at Lexy who backed up a step. "What are *you* doing here?"

Lexy felt like a kid caught with her hand in the cookie jar until she realized she wasn't the only one who wasn't supposed to be there.

"Me? What are the two of *you* doing? I thought I heard you talking about killing Chef Dugasse."

Lexy blurted it out without thinking then realized maybe she shouldn't have said it. If they really were the killers then they'd already killed once and there wasn't much to stop them from killing her. Lexy felt a pang in her stomach as she realized no one knew where she was.

"I didn't say *I* killed the chef, I asked Prescott if *he* killed the chef." Sylvia looked down, noticed her rumpled shirt, turned red and started smoothing it and tucking it in.

"Why would he kill Chef Dugasse?"

Sylvia and Prescott exchanged a look. Lexy wondered if she should make a break for it.

"I wouldn't ... I didn't ... but ..." Prescott stammered.

"What is going on?" Lexy demanded.

Sylvia sighed and turned to Prescott. "We might as well tell her. She's so nosey, she's not going to stop until she finds out the truth and it's better that we give her the real story."

Nosey? Lexy's back stiffened and she raised her eyebrows waiting for the 'real story'.

Sylvia ran her fingers through her blonde hair and looked at Lexy. "You were right about me having an affair."

Lexy's eyebrows shot up. She *knew* it!

"But it wasn't with Dugasse," Sylvia added.

Lexy's eyebrows fell back down and mashed together.

"It was with Prescott." Sylvia turned to Prescott and he nodded.

Lexy felt her mouth fall open. She ping-ponged her eyes back and forth between the two of them. "But why did you act so squirrelly about Dugasse's death?"

Sylvia sighed, collapsing into the guest chair. "Dugasse found out about our affair and he threatened to blackmail us."

"So when he ended up dead ... we each thought the other might have done it," Prescott added.

"So that's why you asked about hiding the body?" Lexy turned to Sylvia. "But why would you think I would want to hide it?"

"I don't know what I was thinking. When I saw him dead, I panicked."

Prescott put his hand on Sylvia's shoulder. "So you see, we were acting strange because we were covering for each other."

Lexy narrowed her eyes. "That's what you *say*, but how do I know the two of you weren't in on it together?"

"We both have alibis."

"You do?"

"Yes," Sylvia said. "Justin was in the freezer at the same time I was that morning. We discussed the way Chef had yelled at Thomas."

"And I was in a meeting with eight other people," Prescott added.

Lexy felt her stomach deflate. Sylvia had been her best suspect and now she'd have to find someone else. But who?

"Hey, what are you doing here this time of night, anyway?" Sylvia interrupted her thoughts.

Lexy felt her cheeks grow warm. "Oh, umm ... well, I caught Brad Meltzer going through Dugasse's office the other day and I wanted to see what he was up to."

"Meltzer? He's been acting really strange since Chef Dugasse died," Sylvia said.

"How so?"

"Like a jerk. I mean he was always kind of a jerk but now with chef gone, he's being rather disrespectful and refusing to do the tasks I give him."

"Do you think he wanted the head chef job?" Prescott asked.

"Maybe. But since I was the sous-chef, he would know that I would be the likely candidate for that job. I can assure you, I won't be making *him* the next sous-chef."

"Maybe he is just upset at Dugasse's passing. He really seemed to adore him," Lexy suggested.

Sylvia pressed her lips together. "I don't know. He followed Dugasse around but he didn't seem to admire him ... It was more like he was stalking him."

"You don't think he had anything to do with Dugasse's murder, do you?" Prescott asked.

"I don't think he could have been the killer," Lexy said. "He was standing right in front of me about the time the chef got murdered. Or shortly after. I would think he'd have had blood on him ... or been unsettled. But he wasn't."

"Well I don't know who could have done it ... if it wasn't you." Sylvia looked pointedly at Lexy.

"It wasn't. You have more of a motive than I do." Lexy's voice rose along with her anger.

"Ladies!" Prescott cut in. "Let's say it wasn't either one of you. Who would have had the strongest motive?"

"Maybe the wife?" Sylvia answered.

"According to Detective Payne, the wife has an alibi," Lexy said.

Sylvia sighed and glanced at Prescott. "I just hope the killer is found soon so people don't dig too deep into the goings on here and find out about us."

Prescott cleared his throat. "Yes, umm ... Lexy. I hope we can keep each other's secrets."

"Secrets?"

Prescott gestured out into the hall. "We won't tell that you were in here after hours looking around if you keep quiet about our relationship."

Lexy stared at the two of them. The last thing she needed was someone telling Payne she was sneaking around in here—it would make her look guilty of something. And since she didn't really care about their affair she figured that was a good deal.

"Sure, I'll keep quiet. But I might need your help."

"With what?"

"Victoria Dugasse said her husband kept sneaking out at night presumably to meet his lover," Lexy said.

Sylvia and Prescott shrugged. "So?"

"I thought he was meeting Sylvia, but if he wasn't, then where was he going and who was he meeting?" Lexy asked.

"I would have no idea." Prescott spread his arms, palms out and shrugged.

"Wait a minute," Sylvia said. "I might."

Lexy raised her brows at the other woman and gestured for her to elaborate.

"A couple of nights ago when I was leaving here after ... umm ... meeting Prescott, I noticed someone cooking in the kitchen. I'm pretty sure it was Dugasse."

Lexy felt her heartbeat kick. "Did you see anyone else with him?"

Sylvia's cheeks turned pink. "I didn't want anyone to know I was here, so I didn't go near the kitchen, but I'm sure I heard him talking in there."

"That's odd. Why would he meet his secret lover in the dining hall kitchen and cook?" Lexy wondered.

"Stranger things have happened," Prescott said. "I can tell you one thing though—if we can figure out who he was meeting, we may have found our killer."

Chapter Fourteen

Lexy cracked one eye open just as the sun was just starting to rise. She closed her eye and rolled over, stretching her back. Feeling the weight of someone staring at her, she opened both her eyes and looked straight into a pair of deep brown orbs which were gazing at her with expectant adoration. Sprinkles.

Lexy felt her lips curl in a smile and reached out to pet the dog who reacted by leaping off the bed and running circles on the floor.

"Okay, okay. I'll get up," Lexy whispered, then swung her legs over the bed.

She padded into the small kitchen, filled Sprinkles' bowl with dog food, then set it down. Lexy leaned against the counter while Sprinkles dug into the food. She was excited to tell Nans what she had learned from Sylvia and Prescott the night before, but it was too early—she wouldn't have time to pop over there before work so it would just have to wait until their meeting at two.

Suddenly in a hurry to get to the kitchen and get her baking done for the day, Lexy grabbed

Sprinkles' leash and dashed outside with the dog who quickly did her business then ran back inside and jumped in bed with Jack.

Her dog duties accomplished, Lexy threw on a tee shirt and jeans, planted a kiss on Jack's sleeping cheek and then headed off to the kitchen.

She hurried up the path, the tantalizing smell of bacon blanketed the resort causing her mouth to water. Slipping inside the back door, she took a detour past the griddle where the bacon was sizzling and grabbed a piece, crunching it into her mouth before continuing on to her area.

She assembled the flour, butter, sugar, baking powder, salt and milk for biscuits she would use as the basis for a strawberry shortcake that would be served for dessert at that evening's dinner. She was just measuring the last of the ingredients into the giant mixing bowl when Sylvia appeared at her side.

"I've done some poking around and no one here knows who would have been in the kitchen late at night," Sylvia said in a low voice.

Lexy glanced around the kitchen. Only about half the staff was in, but she wouldn't have been surprised if no one else admitted to knowing anything either.

"Where's Brad?" Lexy's brow creased as she looked around for the irritating chef.

Sylvia checked her watch. "He's not in yet."

"Oh, well it probably wouldn't help to ask him, but I think we should try to keep an eye on him between the two of us. I'm making up the biscuits and whipped cream for strawberry shortcake, but I have to leave around one thirty," Lexy said.

Sylvia nodded. "I'll keep my eyes and ears open."

"Open for what?" Deena asked as she came up behind them.

A look of panic crossed Sylvia's face.

"Anything that might have to do with Dugasse's murder," Lexy offered, putting Sylvia at ease and answering the teen's question.

"Oh." Deena looked at Sylvia suspiciously. As head chef, Sylvia was probably too much of an authority to be trusted from Deena's point of view and Lexy found herself wishing the other woman would leave. She could see that Deena was bursting at the seams to tell her something.

It must have been Lexy's lucky day because Sylvia turned away from the counter and said, "Well, back to work," as she headed off toward the front of the kitchen.

As soon as Sylvia was out of earshot, Deena whipped her head back around to Lexy. "I may have found something out that will help you."

Lexy felt a flutter of excitement in her stomach. "Great. Let's start this batter up and then get the ingredients for the flavored whipped creams. Then you can tell me."

Lexy indicated for Deena to finish measuring the ingredients into the bowl while she got heavy cream from the fridge. She stopped by the pantry for some sugar and flavored extracts so that she could make some flavored whipped creams for people to put on their strawberry shortcakes. The shortcake, cut up strawberries and whipped cream would be refrigerated separately and then assembled at the last minute before dessert.

She dropped the ingredients on the counter next to the mixer that was already beating the dough.

"These will be easy. We're just going to make three bowls—one vanilla, one coconut and one almond flavored. So we'll just whip the cream, sugar and extract together." Lexy handed the brown vanilla extract bottle to Deena. "You do the vanilla."

Deena followed Lexy's lead, matching her measurements and adding the extract carefully. They picked up their bowls and whisks and started hand whisking the cream.

Lexy raised her eyebrows and glanced around to make sure no one could hear them. "So, what did you find out?"

Deena pressed her lips together, her arm quivering as it worked the cream in the bowl.

"You have to promise not to tell anyone." She looked solemnly at Lexy.

"I promise."

Deena glanced around. "Some of the kids … we hang out on the trails at night. Sometimes we have a bonfire. But anyway, one of them told me that she saw a guy coming up the trail and being let in the back door of the kitchen. And it happened more than once."

Lexy stopped whisking, her heartbeat picking up speed. "What trail?"

"One of the middle ones. Not the one that goes to the parking lot or the one that ends up by the cabins."

"Do you know what time of night?"

Deena made a face and lowered her voice so that it was barely audible. "Don't tell anyone but it was a few hours after midnight ... my friend snuck out of her cabin. Her parents don't know."

Lexy's heart beat even faster—that was the same time Dugasse's wife said he was sneaking off. "Did she say what he looked like?"

"She didn't really have a description. She said he looked big and tough. And one thing was strange."

"What's that?" Lexy's brows creased together as she started whisking the cream again.

"He wore a thick leather jacket—a biker jacket. She said he must have been real hot in that in the middle of summer."

***

Lexy and Deena hurried through making the whipped cream, a batch of blondies and some moon pies. By the time she left it was quarter to two. She rushed down the path to Nans and burst through the front door to find all four women of the *Ladies Detective Club* sitting around the table drinking tea.

Nans peeked at her watch. "How nice of you to join us, I thought maybe you might not make it for our little excursion."

Lexy felt her face flush. "Sorry, I had to finish the baking. But you'll be glad you didn't leave without me because I have some interesting news."

Four sets of gray eyebrows shot up.

"Do tell," Ida said.

"Last night, I went back to the dining hall to look in Dugasse's office," she started.

"Alone?" Helen interrupted.

Lexy felt a twinge. "Yes, I know it was a bit dangerous but I wanted to see if I could figure out what Brad was looking for."

"And did you?"

"Not really, but I found something very interesting."

"What's that?" Nans asked.

"Sylvia Spicer and Prescott Charles," Lexy said, proud of her late night discovery.

"What about them?" Ruth asked.

"They were there ... in the middle of the night ... in secret," Lexy said. "It turns out Sylvia *was* having an affair, but it was with Charles—not Dugasse."

"Ohhhh."

"So, she didn't kill him in a fit of passion?" Ida looked disappointed.

"No," Lexy said. "And they both have alibis that can be corroborated by other people."

"Well, darn. We sure are running out of suspects." Helen went over to the white board and erased Sylvia's name.

"So what was Brad looking for in Dugasse's office?" Nans asked.

"I don't know." Lexy shrugged. "The only thing in there is recipes ... so I was wondering if he could be looking for that famous chili recipe."

"Ha! Things are all starting to point to that chili contest. It usually comes down to money." Ruth shook her head knowingly.

"Maybe ... or maybe not," Lexy said. "I also found out something that might tie the bikers to Dugasse."

"Oh?"

"My assistant told me that the teens hang out in the woods there behind the dining hall and one of her friends said she saw a man that fits the biker's descriptions being let in the back door of the kitchen."

"By Dugasse?"

"She didn't say but it was in the middle of the night about the same time that Dugasse's wife said he was missing from home."

Helen scrunched up her face. "Why would a biker be meeting Dugasse in the middle of the night?"

"Maybe they were having an affair!" Ida wiggled her eyebrows, apparently delighted with the thought.

Lexy scrunched her face together, the image of Dugasse and a burly biker having an affair in the kitchen made her queasy.

"Well, I guess we'll find out soon enough." Nans stood up and went over to the fridge. "Are you guys ready to go make some new friends?"

"I guess so," Lexy said, "but I'm curious ... what is it that you think will get them to talk to us?"

"Why, one of my famous mile high apple pies, of course," Nans said, bending over and grabbing something out of the fridge. She turned around holding out a beautiful golden-crusted apple pie.

"No man alive has ever been able to resist my apple pie, and I'm sure these biker gentlemen are no exception."

Chapter Fifteen

They stopped by Lexy's cottage and Nans got Sprinkles into her harness while Lexy changed clothes.

"Do you have the bracelet that you found on the trail the other day?" Nans asked.

"I think so." Lexy looked around the room for the jeans she had been wearing that day. She found them in a pile on the chair and dug into the front pocket producing the bracelet.

"Here it is." She held it up and Nans reached out and took it.

"You never know when this might come in handy," Nans said, putting it in her pocket. Then she grabbed the pie off the table where she'd set it when they came in and led the way out the front door.

The five of them walked the same path they had the other day. They each took turns holding the pie.

"What, exactly are we hoping to learn from this excursion?" Ida asked and Lexy remembered she hadn't been with them the other day.

"Well, at the end of the path is the biker camp we told you about. In light of the bracelet Lexy found and what Deena told her, it seems pretty likely they are involved or they know something," Nans said handing the pie to Ruth.

"Are they dangerous?" Ida asked.

Lexy chewed her bottom lip. "Well, they did have a knife and a gun ... but they didn't seem too keen to use it on us."

"But they also weren't that happy to see us." Ruth handed the pie to Helen.

"Which is why I baked the pie, to sweeten them up," Nans said.

"Do you think they killed him?" Lexy asked.

"I'm not sure what the motive would be," Nans answered. "But he could have been having an affair with the biker that was visiting him and they had a falling out."

"I can't picture any of those tough bikers being gay." Helen handed the pie to Ida.

"Maybe Dugasse was having an affair with one of the bikers' girlfriends and they had it out over her?" Ruth offered.

"Either way, the best thing to do is just make friends and then use our investigative skills to find out the truth," Nans said taking the pie from Ida.

They got to the clearing where the camp was and Lexy's stomach twisted up in a knot.

The same dog was on the porch and he lifted his head when he heard them approach. Lexy hesitated but Nans forged ahead, walking right up to the door and knocking. Lexy followed, watching as Sprinkles and the Boxer re-acquainted themselves.

The door jerked open and Lexy's heart surged into her throat. A large, bald man growled at them from the other side of the door. Inside Lexy could see five other bikers gathered around a table. She recognized the big guy with the gun from the other day. He came over to the door and peered out at them.

"It's those grandmas!" Another guy said from inside.

The two guys stepped out onto the porch and closed the door behind them.

"What do you want?" The first guy eyed them suspiciously, then glanced over his shoulder at the closed door.

Lexy's heartbeat skittered. *What was he hiding in there?* She could smell something cooking in the air and wondered if they had a meth lab or some other illegal operation going on inside.

"Did *he* send you?" The guy from the other day asked.

"What? No, we told you no one sent us," Nans replied.

"So you aren't in cahoots with that chef?"

Cahoots?

"What chef? Dugasse?" Ruth asked.

The two guys looked at each other. "You know Dugasse?"

Lexy's heart flipped. "We did."

"And you're not from the other chef?"

"Noooo." Nans drew the word out.

One of the guys looked down at the dogs who were laying side by side watching the conversation.

"Looks like our dogs get along like old friends," he said.

Nans shoved the pie up in their faces. "And we just want to be friends, too."

"Is that apple?" the biggest guy asked.

Nans nodded and his eyes lit up. "That's my favorite."

He glanced at the other guy. "Should we let them in?"

The other guy shrugged. "Okay, but if we find out you are up to something you'll be sorry."

He opened the door and they shuffled in. The bikers that were sitting around the table all stood up and a round of introductions ensued. They *seemed* like regular guys ... except for the abundance of leather and tattoos. And the names like Snake, Weasel and Rat.

Lexy gave herself a mental warning not to get too comfortable around them—one of them might have killed Dugasse.

The cabin was one large room with a counter and sink unit on one wall, a big picnic table in the middle, and an old sofa and mismatched chairs on the opposite side of the room. A fridge sat against a wall behind them and a stove was at the end of the counter. One of the guys was at the stove stirring the steaming pots with a wooden spoon.

Nans went to the counter and set her pie down. "Do you guys want a piece? I'm famous for it you know," she said proudly.

Snake and Rat practically fell over themselves getting a knife for her. Nans cut the pie and Rat held out paper plates for her to dish the slices out on. He passed them around with plastic forks and the guys dug in.

Snake rolled his eyes back in his head. "This is so good. Just like my Gam used to make."

"Thanks," Nans said. "You know Lexy here is the baker at the resort. She makes the best desserts. I don't recall ever seeing you guys eating there."

"Oh, this isn't part of the resort," Rat said as he crunched down on a piece of pie crust.

"Oh, it's not?" Nans screwed up her face. "That's funny because I know at least one of you has been to the kitchen."

Everyone stopped chewing and stared at Nans. Lexy's stomach dropped. Her muscles tensed.

"What makes you say that?" Rat asked.

"Well, someone saw one of you walk right down the path and go in through the back door late at night," Nans answered.

The seven guys all looked around at each other. Chairs creaked as they squirmed in their seats.

Nans held up her hands. "Now don't get all nervous. If one of you was having an affair with Dugasse we certainly won't tell."

Snake shot up out of his seat. "What?!"

Lexy's heart leapt and she moved to get between him and Nans.

"I'm not saying any of you killed him," Nans continued, then reached in her pocket. "But we did find this bracelet right at the head of the trail not twenty feet from where he was killed."

"Now you look here old lady," Weasel said advancing on Nans, the veins in his neck straining against his spider web tattoo.

"Wait!" Rat jumped up from his chair and grabbed Weasel's arm.

Weasel shook off Rat's arm. "We can't let her say stuff like that about us."

"It's okay," Rat said holding up his hand. "That bracelet is mine."

"You were the one having an affair with Chef Dugasse?" Ida stared at Rat.

Rat shook his head. "I wasn't having an affair with Dugasse, but I did go there to meet him. Several times."

"But why?" Nans asked.

"Because he was my father," Rat looked down at the ground, his eyes moist. "He was teaching me to cook."

Chapter Sixteen

"Dugasse was your father?" Lexy stared at Rat. "But I didn't even know he had any kids."

"No one knew. We actually just found out a few months ago ourselves when my mother died. They weren't married and she never told me who my father was until right before she passed. The funny thing is, I always wanted to be a chef ..." Rat let his voice trail off, looking out the window toward the path that led to the dining hall.

"A chef?" Ida sized him up.

"Yeah, you don't think bikers have regular jobs? Snake here is an accountant, Weasel's an architect and Stone owns a coffee franchise," he said waving his hand at the others as he talked about them.

Lexy felt her eyes widen as she looked at the men—dirty, unshaven and loaded in leather and tattoos. She couldn't imagine hiring an accountant named Snake or an architect named Weasel.

"These aren't our real names," Snake said catching her incredulous look. "I'm Arty, and that's Devon, James, Zander, Ricky and Rusty. The other names are just our biker nicknames."

"And we clean up real good," Weasel said looking down at himself.

"So you didn't kill Dugasse?" Ruth said to Rat, aka Ricky.

"No, of course not."

Ida let out a sigh of frustration. "Well if it wasn't the wife, and it wasn't Sylvia Spicer and it wasn't one of you, then who the hell *did* kill him?"

Rat rubbed his face with his hand. "That's what *I'd* like to know."

"Did he have any enemies? Did he mention anyone he thought might want to harm him?" Nans asked.

"Well, there was this one other chef that Dad said was threatening him. He wanted to buy Dad's chili recipe for the *Chili Battle* and when Dad refused, he got pretty mad."

"Chef Marchesi?" Ruth asked.

"Yes, that's him!" Rat narrowed his eyes at her. "How do you know him?"

"We don't." Ruth shook her head. "But we heard he was a rival for the chili contest and Payne mentioned him as a possible suspect."

"Is that who you thought sent us?" Lexy asked.

"Yes. We knew he wanted to get his hands on the recipe and thought he might send someone to try and take it ... but we thought it would be by force, not with pies." Snake chuckled.

"And you guys have the recipe?" Nans raised her brows.

Rat nodded. "Dad and I were going to enter the chili contest together but now that he's gone, I'll enter it myself ... in his honor."

"We're cooking up a test run now." Snake pointed to the stove. "Would you like a taste?"

Nans went over to the stove, lifted one of the lids and stuck her nose in. "Oh, this smells good."

Snake and Weasel handed out bowls and everyone lined up at the stove where Rat proudly ladled out the chili.

Lexy took her bowl over by the window and brought the spoon tentatively to her lips. It *was* good—sweet and with just enough of a spicy kick.

"This is delicious," Ida said.

"Umm." Helen, Ruth and Nans agreed.

"I don't get why this Marchesi guy would kill Rat's dad over a chili recipe," Snake said.

"Well, everyone seems to think Dugasse's chili would win the contest and winning that contest could be worth millions." Nans slurped the rest of her chili.

"Millions?" Rat's eyebrows mashed together.

"Yeah, your father didn't tell you?"

"No. He just seemed happy that we were working on something together," Rat said looking even sadder than before.

"The good news is that now *you* might be the one to win that contest," Helen said.

"And the millions," Ruth added.

"Unless Marchesi gets to you first," Nans cautioned.

"We can't be certain he's the killer," Lexy said.

"No, but he certainly had a motive," Nans replied. "And right now he's the best candidate we have. We just have to prove he did it."

"How can you do that?" Rat asked.

Nans shrugged. "We've caught killers before. Usually we just snoop around and something always comes up. I don't see why this would be any different."

Ida turned to Rat. "What time do you start setting up for the *Chili Battle*?"

"We get our assigned spots tomorrow night and we can set up our tables and canopies then," Rat said.

"The next day, the contest grounds open at noon. We can start cooking then and the general public is allowed in around 4 pm," Snake added.

"Boy, it sure would be great to get in early and snoop around his tent," Ruth said.

Rat looked at her and snapped his fingers. "I know! You can meet us tomorrow night and we'll get you in with V.I.P. visitor passes ... if you want."

"Oh that would be perfect!" Nans put her chili bowl in the sink and started washing the dishes.

"Oh, hey, you don't have to do that ... you're a guest." Snake took over the job of dish washing and Nans raised her brows at Lexy who shrugged.

"I feel much better knowing you guys are helping find out who killed my dad," Rat said. "I didn't have a lot of confidence in that detective Payne."

"Neither do we, actually," Nans replied.

"So he knows about you then." Lexy cut her eyes to Rat.

"Yes, he was here the other day," Rat said. "Weasel's cousin is on the police force here but he didn't know I was Dugasse's son. I guess Payne figured that out on his own somehow."

Lexy raised a brow. Maybe Payne wasn't as much of a bumbling idiot as he appeared to be.

"Well, I guess we better get going." Ida pushed herself up from the table where she'd found a seat in between Stone and Rusty.

Lexy noticed the men exchanging a look and her muscles tensed. *What was that about?*

Rat raised his eyebrows at Snake and Snake nodded.

"Is something wrong?" Lexy ventured, her nerves on high alert.

"No ... we just ..." Rat looked at the others. "Should we?"

"Should you what?" Nans stood near the door, her hand on the knob.

"Yeah, go ahead." Snake and the others nodded at Rat.

"Well, I was wondering if you ladies would like to go with us to biker bingo tonight ... it's a lot of fun, the biker camps from all around the lake go and tonight's the big game where you can win the grand prize."

"Oh, that sounds like fun!" Nans raised her brows at the other ladies. "Do you want to go?"

Ruth, Ida and Helen nodded. The women loved bingo and never passed up a chance to get in on a big game.

"What's the grand prize?" Ida asked.

Snake's eyes lit up. "A Harley."

"Count me in!" Ruth said. "I always wanted a Harley."

Chapter Seventeen

Lexy didn't go to biker bingo. Partly because she wanted to spend the time with Jack, but mostly because she didn't want to have to explain to him how they'd befriended a gang of bikers. He'd been really understanding about her crime solving activities on this trip and she didn't want to push her luck.

Jumping into the shower, she washed her hair then fluffed it dry letting the natural wave take over before changing into a short turquoise colored sundress. By the time Jack got back from fishing, she had beer in the cooler, steaks on the grill and Jack's favorite coconut cream pie in the fridge which was, strangely enough, located on the porch.

She was sitting in one of the rockers on their screened-in porch enjoying the view of the lake through the trees when Jack joined her, fresh from the shower. He'd given his hair a rough towel dry so it stuck up around his unshaven face. The rumpled hair and stubble gave him a handsome bad-boy look, causing Lexy's pulse to beat a little faster.

She handed him a beer from the cooler and he sank into the second rocker. Sprinkles adjusted her position so that she was lying on the floor in between the two rocking chairs and Jack bent down to scratch behind her ears.

"How was fishing today?" Lexy asked, hoping the subject of fishing would distract Jack enough so he didn't ask about *her* day.

"Good. I caught a four pound bass, which beat Norman's best catch of three point eight pounds." Jack smiled. "Plus a few smaller bass and some pickerel."

"You're really getting into vacation mode ... too bad we only have a few more days here."

"Yep. I haven't relaxed this much on vacation in years. But it will be good to get back home and back to work." Jack ran his finger lightly up Lexy's arm sending tingly shivers down her spine. "Until we go on our next vacation ... just the two of us."

"Next vacation?" Lexy's eyebrows mashed together.

Jack tilted his head at her. "Our honeymoon? We *are* getting married, right?"

Lexy laughed. "Oh, sorry. Yes, of course ... but I guess there's a lot of planning before that can happen."

"Well, I think you should start planning right away, as soon as we get back."

Lexy's heart lifted at the thought. They'd been engaged for several months, now, but sometimes it seemed like Jack might be having second thoughts. He sounded so sure about it now that Lexy figured she'd just been acting silly and vowed to put the plans into action right away.

"How is the Dugasse case going?" Jack pulled her out of her thoughts.

"Well, it wasn't the wife." Lexy watched Jack pad out to the grill in his bare feet and flip the steaks over. The smell of grilling meat combined with the sizzling sound they made when he flipped them caused her mouth to water.

"How do you know?" he asked through the screen.

"Payne said she had an alibi."

"He shared information with you?"

"Only by accident." Lexy grimaced. "He came to the kitchen to lecture me about bothering suspects and let it slip that the wife wasn't the killer."

"Well that sounds familiar." Jack returned to his rocker and laughed as he settled back in with his beer. "So do you think it was the other chef ... Sylvia?"

"She wasn't having the affair with him and she also has an alibi." Lexy felt a pang of guilt in not telling Jack the whole story about Sylvia's affair with Prescott Charles but it wasn't relevant to the murder case and she'd promised not to tell.

"So you're out of suspects?" Jack raised a brow at Lexy, then grabbed the platter and headed out to the grill.

"No, we have one other." Lexy got up and started setting out plates and a salad on the small table they had set up for eating on.

"Who is this other suspect?" Jack prompted as he dished steaks onto their plates.

Lexy glanced out the window to make sure no one else was around. "Another chef—one who was threatening Dugasse about his chili recipe."

Jack's eyebrows shot up. "I didn't know he was getting threats. That sounds like something to investigate. I hope Payne is aware of that."

"I'm sure he is." Lexy put a small chunk of steak in her mouth and it practically melted on her tongue. She rolled her eyes back in her head. "Nummy ... this is sooo good."

Sprinkles put her paw on Lexy's foot and stared at her as if to say "don't forget to give me some." Lexy's heart surged and she threw her a small piece.

"Anyway," Lexy said. "Dugasse's son said this Marchesi guy—that's the other chef—tried to buy the chili recipe and when Dugasse refused he got mad."

"Wait ... Dugasse has a son?"

Lexy nodded. "Yeah, I guess it was kind of a secret ..." She let her voice trail off not wanting to get into the details of how *she* found out about the son.

"Speaking of the chili recipe ... are we going to the big *Chili Battle* tomorrow night?" Jack asked.

"Of course. It should be interesting, considering what happened to Dugasse." Lexy purposely forgot to tell him about Dugasse's son entering the contest with the recipe.

"That's for sure. And I heard there were going to be fireworks after. How about we bring a big blanket and spread it out on the hill? We can gorge ourselves on chili and then lay back and watch the fireworks."

"Sounds good." Lexy's stomach flipped wondering how she'd manage to eat chili with Jack and stalk Marchesi at the same time.

Jack finished off the last of his steak and salad, then took a long pull on his beer.

"The thing is, I'm not really sure how to go about getting clues that prove Marchesi is the killer," Lexy said, wiping her plate clean and stacking it on top of Jack's.

Jack leaned back and took another sip of beer. "I would try to establish a timeline ... where was Marchesi when the murder happened? Do you think he did it himself or did he have an accomplice?"

Lexy pursed her lips. "I don't know, I hadn't thought about it."

"One technique we like to use is to simply follow and observe ... we do it with suspects or people that seem to know too much about the case. Usually something shakes out. Criminals like that are dumb and all it takes is watching them a bit to find a clue."

Lexy settled back in her chair. She'd have to have Ruth find out where Marchesi was staying and then maybe one of them could follow him around while Lexy was working tomorrow morning.

"But you need to be careful if you follow this guy around ... he could be a killer. You'd be smart to leave that part to Payne." Jack's eyes drilled into hers as if he was reading her thoughts.

"Oh, of course," she said, then stood up and walked to the fridge, thinking to distract him from giving her the usual lecture about messing in police business with his favorite coconut cream pie.

She opened the door, enjoying the blast of cool air. "I have your favorite pie for dessert," she said, looking at him over the top of the door.

Jack got up and walked over to her, pulling her out from behind the door and closing it. He slid his arm around her waist, dragging her to him. He dipped his head, his lips brushing lightly against hers.

"Actually, I had something else in mind for dessert."

Chapter Eighteen

Lexy was halfway through frosting a batch of miniature cupcakes when Nans, Ruth, Ida and Helen showed up in the kitchen the next morning. She glanced nervously out the window, half expecting to see a shiny new Harley in the parking lot.

"How was biker bingo? Did you guys win anything?"

"Ida won a hundred dollars, Helen got a gift certificate for a pedicure and Ruth and I got skunked." Nans shook her head.

Lexy made a face. "A gift certificate for a pedicure? Who would have thought bikers would want that as a prize?"

Nans shrugged. "I guess one of the bikers has a salon and he donated it."

"So you didn't win the Harley?" Lexy eyed Ruth.

"No." Ruth laughed. "I guess I'll have to make do with my Oldsmobile."

"Probably safer," Lexy offered.

"For everyone," Helen added and Nans and Ida snickered.

"But we did get the V.I.P. passes," Ruth said to Lexy. "We're supposed to meet Snake, Rat and the gang at the field around five."

"Okay." Lexy checked her watch. "I'm tied up here this morning but I was thinking it might be smart to follow Marchesi around today. If he is the killer and he's still after the recipe, he might do something suspicious."

"Good idea. I'm sure he must be in town by now for the contest," Ida said.

"Did you ever look into that?" Nans asked Ruth.

"Not yet. Shouldn't be too hard though." Ruth leaned in and said in a low voice, "I have a great program that hacks the hotel guest databases."

"Easy peasy. We'll just find out where he is then stake out his hotel and put a tail on him if he leaves." Lexy thought Nans looked quite pleased that she'd been able to fit lots of police jargon in that sentence.

"Okay, but don't confront him. He could be dangerous," Lexy said, then wondered if she'd been listening to Jack too much.

A splash of vibrant color at the front of the kitchen caught her eye and her heart sank when she saw Detective Payne in a bright pink shirt and pink, white and blue plaid shorts making his way down the aisle toward her.

"What is it?" Nans turned to see what was causing the look of distaste on Lexy's face. "Oh. Well, time for us to go."

Nans, Ruth, Ida and Helen turned abruptly and scooted off in the other direction before Lexy even had time to say good-bye.

Payne smiled at the cupcakes, then frowned at Lexy. "Miss Baker, I hear you've been making the rounds."

"The rounds?" Lexy tried on her best wide-eyed innocent look. "I have no idea what you mean."

Payne narrowed his eyes at her then grabbed a little cupcake and shoved the whole thing in his mouth. He brought the spiral notebook and pencil out of his pocket.

"I think you know we have a new suspect," he said, studying her reaction. A glob of blue frosting rested on the corner of his mouth.

Lexy raised an eyebrow. She didn't point out the frosting.

"It seems Dugasse had a son," Payne announced.

"I knew that," Lexy said. "But the son didn't kill him."

"Oh really? And how do you know that?"

Lexy pressed her lips together. She was already in enough trouble with Payne and didn't want to tell him she'd scouted out the biker camp on her own or that she'd found the bracelet at the head of the trail.

"Rumors around the kitchen." She waved her hand around the room.

Payne looked at the ceiling and tapped the eraser end of his pencil on his lips. The glob of frosting quivered but stayed in place.

"Seems like you know an awful lot about this murder ... for someone who isn't really involved."

Lexy's stomach sank. Whenever she talked to Payne she seemed to get herself in more trouble. All the more reason to investigate this herself, she thought.

Payne picked another cupcake off the tray and shoved it in his mouth. This one with chocolate frosting. "I trust you'll be going to the *Chili Battle*?"

Lexy nodded. *What an odd thing for him to ask.*

"Good, then all my favorite suspects will be in the same area at once."

And with that he turned and walked off leaving Lexy to wonder what he meant.

***

The fairgrounds at Lakeshore Resort where the *Chili Battle* was being held was a giant field with barns at one end. Today, a big section was roped off and Lexy could see canopies being set up in rows. Two men in khaki shirts guarded the entrance.

Nans pulled the V.I.P. passes out of her giant purse and handed them out so each of them could show their ticket and be let inside. Since the event wasn't open for the general public, there wasn't a lot of people, but those that were there seemed to be quite busy.

It was sectioned off into booths each about ten by twenty and with a post that held boxy electrical outlets. The contestants were setting up their tents and tables and getting their cookware in order. Lexy remembered that Rat had said they weren't allowed to start cooking until noon tomorrow. She figured most of the contestants wanted to make sure they had everything in good order tonight so they could get right into cooking first thing the next day.

"So you didn't find out anything today when you followed Marchesi?" Lexy said once they were far enough away from anyone who might overhear.

"No," Nans said. "It was boring. Helen fell asleep in the back seat."

"He stayed in the hotel and went out once to the grocery store. Bought a lot of beans," Ida added.

"But you got a good look at him, right? So you'll recognize him if you see him here."

"Oh we got a good look," Nans said, craning her neck to scan the area. "But I don't see him here."

"How about we go logically down the rows and check out each booth?" Ruth asked.

"Okay, we'll start at this end." Lexy pointed to a booth in the corner. "Then go up and down the rows."

They started toward the end and Lexy felt a tingle at the base of her neck. *Was someone watching her?* She turned around but didn't see anyone. Probably just nerves about what might happen if they have a run-in with Marchesi, she thought.

They walked the rows methodically. Lexy noticed a lot of the contestants had special canopies with their names. Probably not unusual considering the amount of money at stake. She wondered if some of them were professional contestants or just people that liked to make chili.

Nans stopped in front of a booth that had a tropical looking canopy with "Chilin' Chili" written on it in scrolly letters. The canopy was turquoise and pink and the contestants inside had matching aprons. Even their crock pots were turquoise.

"This looks like a fun booth," Nans said.

One of the aproned contestants smiled over at Nans. "It is. We even give out small margarita samples." She nodded to the stack of cups.

A second lady glanced up. "Be sure to come back tomorrow for the tasting ... and vote for us!"

Nans winked at Lexy as they continued down the row. "I know the first place I'll be heading to tomorrow night."

They passed more interesting booths. "Hot to Taught" was manned by teachers and "It's a

Gas" claimed to have the hottest—and gassiest—chili in the contest.

As they walked the rows, Lexy couldn't shake the feeling of being watched. She kept looking behind her, but didn't see anyone.

They found Rat, Snake and the others in a booth in the third row. Nans rushed right over and Lexy watched the four older women exchange high-fives with the six bikers.

Lexy noticed their tent was a plain white color with Dugasse written in script on an awning that hung on the front. The guys wore plain black aprons and Rat shuffled around inside, placing items in one spot, then moving them a few seconds later.

"What's that for?" Ruth asked pointing to a large grill they had set up in the corner.

"We're going to warm the cornbread up on it so it will be lightly grilled." Rat smiled proudly. "It's going to be the best cornbread in the contest."

"Over here we have the crockpots ... this is where we'll start the beans in the secret sauce right at noon." Snake pointed to a table with rows of mismatched crockpots on it. Lexy wondered if the boys had attended every yard sale in a ten mile radius to amass the odd collection.

"And over here we'll cook up the meat." Weasel walked over to a stove plate that sat on another table.

"Then we mix it all together with vegetables and put it back in the crockpot to simmer for a few hours," Rat said.

"Sounds like you guys have it all worked out." Nans looked around the booth, then lowered her voice. "Have you seen Marchesi?"

"No, we were afraid he might come by and bother us, but nothing so far. I'm not sure he even knows who we are." Rat shrugged.

"But if he tries anything, he'll be sorry," Snake said, pointing to a stack of baseball bats in the corner.

"I heard his booth was in the very last row," Rat said.

"We should go check it out. He doesn't know who we are so maybe we can interrogate him and get him to slip up," Ida said.

Lexy mashed her brows together. "Interrogate him? That might not be such a good idea."

"Oh, I didn't mean in an obvious way, dear," Ida said. "You know us old ladies have a way of interrogating people without them realizing it."

Lexy gave a half nod. She had to admit, being an octogenarian did have its advantages, one of which was that people paid little attention to what you asked and tended to spill their guts before they even realized what they were saying.

Nans clapped her hands together and started toward the aisle. "Shall we?"

Ruth, Ida, Helen and Lexy said a quick good-bye to the bikers and followed her out. She made her way down to the end of the row and skipped over the next one heading straight for the last row of booths. Lexy followed along, ignoring the feeling that she was being watched.

She rounded the corner to see Nans standing in front of one of the booths.

"Here it is." Nans pointed up at the awning which said Marchesi in block letters along with a black and white line drawing of the chef.

"No one is here." Ida looked deflated.

Lexy glanced around. The booth was blocked off, with tables set up around the edges where one would normally enter. The back had tables too and those were loaded with high tech stainless steel crockpots and racks of spices. On one of the tables close to them was a picture of Marchesi in his chef's uniform in the kitchen.

Lexy picked up the picture. "So this is him?"

Nans looked over her shoulder. "Yep. Looks like he's in his restaurant or something."

"Who's that other guy next to him?" Helen asked.

"I don't know ... wait a minute." Nans grabbed the picture from Lexy and held it close to her face.

"It couldn't be ..." Her voice trailed off as she set the picture down and dug in her purse. She produced something wrapped in a tissue, her eyes lighting up as she unwrapped the tissue and looked inside.

"It is!"

"Is what?" Lexy asked.

Nans laid the object flat in her palm and Lexy recognized it as the bloodied scrap of fabric she'd found under the dumpster.

"The pattern on this fabric matches the pattern on that guy's shirt in the picture ... exactly." Nans emphasized the last word by stabbing her index finger at the man standing next to Marchesi in the picture.

Lexy squinted, comparing the two fabrics and her stomach lurched ... Nans was right.

Ida gasped her eyes riveting between the scrap of fabric and the picture. "That's it! He's the killer!"

***

"Shhh!" Nans looked at Ida. "This doesn't *prove* that he's the killer ... just that he has the same shirt."

"Actually, we don't even know that swatch is *from* the killer," Lexy said.

"It could have been there before the murder," Ruth reminded them.

"We probably shouldn't have taken it." Lexy's stomach sank. "Now Payne will have no way to tie this to the scene of the crime."

"Yeah, it's unlikely that he'll believe us if we suddenly come forward and say we found it there," Ruth said.

"Maybe the best thing to do is to give this to Weasel. He had a cousin on the police force. He might know what to do about it."

Nans frowned down at the swatch. "Yeah, probably. I guess we'll just have to find some other evidence or get Marchesi to admit to it."

"Too bad we couldn't catch him trying to steal the recipe or threatening Rat and the gang."

"Does he even know that Rat is Dugasse's son?"

"Not according to what Rat said earlier," Lexy answered.

"So, for all we know, he thinks he's got the contest all tied up since Dugasse is dead," Ruth said.

"Which is good because when killers think they are in the clear, they tend to let their guard down," Ida added.

"Well, let's get this swatch back to Weasel." Nans wrapped the fabric back in the tissue and put it in her purse. "We can come back to the booth tomorrow when Marchesi is sure to be here and see if we can get him to admit to being the killer ... or at least having his henchman do it."

As they turned to head back down the aisle, Lexy's heart jolted when she caught a glimpse of someone ducking out of sight at the end of the row.

"Hey! You!" She ran toward the person but when she got to the end no one was there—just a crowd of people milling about the area looking in the various booths.

"Damn!" She stopped and waited for Nans and the ladies to catch up.

"What is it?" Nans asked.

"I thought I saw someone watching us." Lexy stood on her tip toes scanning the crowd. "I've had the feeling someone has been following us all night."

Nans pursed her lips together. "Interesting … why would someone follow us?"

Lexy shrugged. "I don't know, but I'm willing to bet it has something to do with Dugasse's murder."

Chapter Nineteen

Lexy kept herself busy the next day making extra batches of brownies and cupcakes to keep her mind off the chili contest that night. She was jittery with the feeling that *something* was going to happen and a little nervous at what Nans might do to try to expose Marchesi.

She'd expected detective Payne to show up and read her the riot act about the swatch of fabric. The bikers had been happy to hear about how they had found it and the picture that showed Marchesi's friend wearing it. Weasel had even whipped out his cell phone and tried to call his cousin on the spot, except there'd been no cell phone service.

Payne hadn't graced the kitchen with his appearance by the time Lexy was done with her kitchen duties and she breathed a sigh of relief. She didn't know if that meant he just didn't know about it yet or if she was off the hook, but either way she wasn't going to have to deal with him today ... at least not until they could get a confession or some other clue from Marchesi later on that night.

Rushing to her cottage to change, Lexy wondered how she was going to get away from Jack to go to the Marchesi booth. Jack wouldn't approve of Nans interrogating him and she certainly wasn't going to let Nans and the ladies go without her. God only knew what kind of trouble they could get into.

She showered and changed into a blue tank top and faded jeans. She fed Sprinkles and dug out a big blanket for them to sit on to view the fireworks which were supposed to start shortly after dark.

Lexy felt the corners of her lips curl in a smile thinking of how romantic it would be to lay on the blanket with Jack and watch the fireworks ... and also of how leaving Jack on the blanket to 'save their spot' would provide the perfect excuse for her venturing off with Nans.

***

By the time Jack finished showering, Nans, Ruth, Helen, Ida and Ida's fiancé Norman had come to collect them. They put Sprinkles in her harness and then they all started off toward the field.

"I figure Norman and Jack can get some chili and then save our spots on the blankets." Ida winked at Lexy. Apparently the older woman had the same idea Lexy did.

They made their way into the event and walked around to a few booths. Lexy wasn't surprised when Nans went straight to the "Chilin Chili" booth and grabbed margaritas for everyone. The salty tang of the drink flirted with Lexy's taste buds as the pungent tequila soothed her nerves.

The air was filled with a festive vibe and the smell of spices. Lexy felt good walking hand in hand with Jack and surrounded by her grandmother and friends, but she still couldn't shake that niggling feeling that she was being followed.

"It's getting crowded up on the hill." Ida pointed to the hillside which was starting to fill up. "Why don't you and Jack grab some chili, then take the blankets and save us a seat? Us girls wanna walk around a little more."

"Okay by you?" Norman asked Jack who nodded. Jack and Norman both loved fishing and the two of them had spent most of the vacation doing just that and becoming close friends in the process.

Lexy knew Jack wasn't much for milling around in crowds so he was more than happy to take the blanket and Sprinkles and set out for more spacious territory. He gave Lexy a quick peck on the cheek and off they went.

"Now, let's get down to business," Nans whispered after they were out of hearing range. She turned and walked briskly toward the very last row where Marchesi's booth was. Taking a detour to breeze by Rat's booth, she stopped only long enough to wish him good luck, then continued on to the last row.

Lexy felt a jolt of apprehension as they turned into the last row. The crowd had thinned and it made her feel exposed. She got that hair standing up feeling on the back of her neck again and wished she'd had two—or more—margaritas.

Her heartbeat picked up speed as they approached the Marchesi tent. The crowd seemed oddly disinterested in it which was strange considering Marchesi was supposed to have one of the best chili recipes. As they got up closer to the tent, Lexy found out why.

The tent was closed.

"What the heck?" Nans turned around to face them her arms extended at her sides, palms out.

"Is anyone in there?" Lexy tried to lift one of the flaps but the tent was buttoned up tight as a drum. She managed to lift a corner flap to get a peek inside.

"It's empty." She shrugged at Nans and the ladies.

"Well, where could he be?" Ruth looked around.

"Maybe out killing someone else that he thinks might steal the win from him," Ida whispered.

"Let's look inside." Nans tugged on the corner of the flap that Lexy had opened and a few more snaps unsnapped making the opening big enough for them to squeeze in.

Lexy's heart pounded against her ribs as she followed Nans inside. She looked around at the tables—crockpots were simmering and the tent smelled deliciously like molasses and spices. She noticed Chef Marchesi had all the most expensive equipment from the stainless steel crockpots to the high tech convection ovens. Everything was top notch right down to the premium mahogany handled knife set.

Lexy's stomach lurched and she sucked in a breath as she stared at the knife set ... the handles were identical to the knife she'd seen sticking out of Dugasse's chest.

"What is it?" Nans turned to her.

"This knife set—it matches the one that killed Dugasse." Lexy pointed to the set. "And it's missing the chef's knife."

"It's too bad you're so nosey."

Lexy whirled toward the sound of the familiar voice, her heart jerking in her chest when she saw who it was.

Brad Meltzer ... and he had a gun pointed right at Nans.

Chapter Twenty

Lexy's heart hammered in her chest. Too late, she realized they'd made a mistake coming into the closed off tent—no one could see them. But would they hear her over the din of the event if she screamed?

"Don't even think about screaming or the old lady gets it," Brad said as if reading her mind.

"Old lady?" Nans bristled at Brad.

"Shut it!

Brad let out a low whistle and a flap on the other side of the tent opened. A large man wheeled in dollies stacked with boxes and burlap sacks. Lexy's blood froze when she recognized him as the man with the plaid shirt in the picture—the killer.

Nans, Ida, Ruth and Helen stood frozen in their tracks

Lexy's heart jerked as Brad started toward the ladies. She lunged toward Brad to prevent him from getting to them, but plaid shirt came at her from the left. She turned to the left, leaping at him to catch him off guard but he lowered his head and smashed into her mid-section sending her plummeting to the ground.

She kicked out and heard a grunt as her foot connected with hard bone. His knee. It merely slowed him for a second and he reached out and grabbed her by the hair, pulling her head back.

Lexy felt his arm squeeze around her neck as her clouding vision registered Brad advancing on Nans and the ladies. She struggled against him but he was like a brick house.

She tried to cry out for Brad not to hurt Nans but the hold on her throat was too tight.

And then everything went dark.

***

Lexy opened her eyes but she couldn't see a thing.

She was rolled up in something and she was moving. Then, the movement stopped. She strained to hear something—anything—that would give her a clue as to where she was but all she could hear was the sound of her heart thumping in her ears and heavy clanking metal. Like chains.

Next thing she knew she was falling, a fall which ended in an explosion of pain in her right shoulder and hip. Then the sound of a door slamming shut and more metal clanking.

Where was she?

She tried to sit up but was restrained by whatever it was that held her. She wiggled, feeling the coarse fabric that was loosely around her. Raising her hands up, she realized she wasn't rolled up in something … she was in a burlap sack!

Fumbling for the top, she managed to push it open and poke her head through. She was in what looked like some sort of dark, windowless shack. She could barely make out four large sacks lying beside her.

Nans!

She wriggled out of her sack and ran over to the one beside her. She could hear grunts from inside and see movement—at least they were alive. She undid the strings and looked in.

"Where the hell are we?" Nans blinked up at her.

"I have no idea. In some building."

"Hey, help me out of here," A muffled voice said from one of the other sacks and Lexy rushed over to free Ruth while Nans unwrapped Ida. Helen managed to get out of hers by herself and they all stood looking around.

"What is this place?" Ruth asked.

"Anyone have a light?"

Helen rummaged in her purse, producing a box of matches. Lexy took them, striking one against the side. The smell of sulfur spiced the air and the match provided a swatch of light which Lexy used to look around the place.

"It's some sort of storage shed." She walked toward the rows of shelving looking at the boxes. Bringing the match closer to a box, she read the writing ... her heart seized and she dropped the match stepping on it as fast as she could.

"Shit!"

"Lexy, dear. There's no need for that kind of language," Nans said.

"This place is full of fireworks! I could have blown us up." Lexy's hand shook as she picked up the match.

"Oh, this must be where they store the fireworks. I think the ones they are using for tonight are already set up though so these must be extra," Ruth said.

"Why do you think they brought us here?" Ida asked.

"I heard Brad say something about getting us out of the way until after the contest when they can dispose of us." Helen rubbed her hands on her upper arms.

"Well, I don't know about you guys, but I'm not going to wait for them to come and *dispose* of us," Nans said.

"Let's see if we can ram the door open." Ruth went over to the door and pushed her shoulder against it. It didn't budge.

"Let me try." Lexy took a few running steps and leapt into the door. It opened a tiny crack, but the door was solid and secured by something. She remembered the sound of metal chains.

"I think it's chained shut. We'll never get it open." Lexy felt her stomach drop. How were they going to get out of there?

Lexy pressed her ear to the door. She couldn't hear anything.

"Does anyone know how far we are from the field?"

A chorus of "no's" answered her.

She pounded on the door. "Help!"

Ida stared at her. "Lexy, I doubt anyone can hear us. The killers aren't *that* stupid ... are they?"

"Wait a minute." Nans turned around and squinted at the shelves. "Gimme those matches ... I want to see what we have to work with here."

"No way. You could blow this thing sky high and us with it!" Lexy shoved the match box into her pocket.

"How about we just use the flashlight app on my cell phone?" Ruth held out her phone and everyone stared at her.

Lexy felt her eyebrows shoot up to her hairline. "You have a cellphone? We can just call someone for help!"

"Oh right." Ruth fiddled with the phone. "Ughh ... no cell service."

"Damn!"

"Shine the flashlight over here," Nans said.

Ruth pointed the end of her cell phone at the shelf and a beam of light illuminated the boxes. Nans walked down the rows, telling Ruth where to point. Finally she found a box she liked and picked some firecrackers out of it, then brought them back to the front of the shed.

"Ida do you have a tube of lipstick?" Nans asked.

"Sure." Ida rummaged in her purse, then produced a gold colored metal lipstick.

"Thanks," Nans said. "Does anyone have any duct tape?"

Helen reached into her purse. "Right here."

Nans grabbed the duct tape and Lexy watched in fascination as she ripped the lipstick out of its container and threw it on the floor.

"Hey, what are you doing?" Ida frowned down at the lipstick. "That's my favorite shade—coral passion."

"All for a good cause," Nans said as she ripped open the fireworks pouring the powder into the lipstick container top, then jamming the bottom on. "Lexy, see if you can find a nail and something hard to pierce a hole in this."

"Oh, I have some nails in my purse," Ruth offered.

Lexy found a large rock in the corner and set the lipstick on the floor. She took a nail from Ruth and balanced it on top, then bashed it with the rock to pierce through the metal.

"Perfect." Nans ripped off some duct tape with her teeth and used it to seal the tube closed, then she threaded the fuse from the fireworks into the hole Lexy had made in the top.

Nans held the modified lipstick out to show them. "Well, who wants to light it?"

"Light it? That thing could blow us up!" Lexy stepped back.

Nans waved her hand. "Oh, don't be silly. There's not a lot in here. I figure we wedge it in the crack of the door and it will be enough to blow the lock off and we can get out of here."

Lexy felt her stomach drop as she looked at Ruth, Ida and Helen. It sounded dangerous to her, but waiting around for Brad and plaid shirt seemed pretty dangerous too.

"Okay." she shrugged and cracked the door open. "Stick it in."

Nans stuck the lipstick in the crack and Lexy let go so the force of the door would hold it in place.

"You guys stand back." She motioned to the other side of the room as she took the matches from her pocket.

Holding her breath, she struck the match then backed up as far away from the lipstick as she could while still being able to touch the match to the fuse. Her heart leapt into her throat as it caught and she ran back to where Nans and the ladies were huddled. She turned away from the door and covered her ears.

Boom!

The door blew open and the five of them tumbled out of the shack coughing and batting at the thick smoke that hung in the air.

Lexy tilted her head to the side, trying to get the ringing in her ears to stop. It started to subside, but was replaced with a low drone which got louder and louder until she realized what it was ... motorcycles!

Rat, Snake, Weasel, Bug and Spike came roaring out of the woods behind them.

"Get on! Marchesi's getting away!"

Lexy looked at Nans and the ladies who shrugged and then hopped on the back of the motorcycles as they raced off in the direction of the chili contest.

Lexy looked back over her shoulder as they sped off and her heart clenched.

"The shed door, it's on fire!" she shouted.

Rat glanced back over his shoulder but kept racing forward. "We don't have time to go back. Marchesi's making a run for it!"

Chapter Twenty One

Lexy felt the sting of bugs smacking her face as they raced over to a wooded patch directly behind Marchesi's tent. As they approached, she could see the fat chef, Brad and the guy in the plaid shirt making a run across the field toward the woods.

Something moved at the edge of the contest area and Lexy's eyes widened when she saw Detectives Payne and Wells racing across the field along with another uniformed officer after Marchesi.

Rat and the gang pushed their bikes to go even faster and Lexy felt her heartbeat racing along with her as they gained on the chef.

Marchesi was getting closer to the woods but Payne was gaining ground as Lexy and the bikers flew out into the clearing. They aimed their bikes toward Marchesi who jerked his head over his shoulder in their direction, his mouth forming a surprised 'O' as he saw the five motorcycles racing toward him.

With a final push, the motorcycles flew across the field and circled around Marchesi and his accomplices preventing their escape.

Marchesi dodged and weaved trying to make it to the woods but the bikes were too quick for him and cut him off at every turn.

And then, just when Lexy thought she'd seen it all, Detective Payne made a running leap. He flew through the air in a colorful blur of pastel shirt and plaid pants, landing right on Marchesi and bringing the big chef to the ground.

Wells and the uniformed officer wrestled with Brad and the third man while Payne whipped out his handcuffs and locked them on Marchesi's wrist.

"Chef Martino Marchesi ... you're under arrest for the murder of Alain Dugasse."

Lexy jumped off the bike and approached Payne. "So, he really is the killer?"

"Not the actual killer, but the mastermind behind it." Payne turned to Brad and the other man. "And those are his accomplices."

"So one of them killed Dugasse?"

Payne nodded. "Marchesi sent Brad to work in the kitchen in order to get close to Dugassc and try to get the recipe. When it became clear that wasn't going to work, and Marchesi's threats didn't scare the chef, Brad lured Dugasse out to the dumpster somehow where the other gentleman was waiting to kill him."

Lexy felt a shiver despite the warm weather. The killer had been out there lurking behind the dumpster that morning and anyone could have stumbled across him.

"I think Brad might have been trying to frame you for it," Payne said to Lexy.

"Yeah, and for a while it seemed like you were going to believe him." Lexy narrowed her eyes at Payne. "So how did you figure out what really happened?"

"Actually, it was all thanks to you." Payne stood, heaving Marchesi up off the ground. "After our talk the other day, I had you followed ... you led us right to the clues in Marchesi's tent."

"The knife set?"

"Yep, that and the scrap of fabric your grandmother found tied the whole case together. Then we just waited for him to come back to the tent here to arrest him. He ran as soon as he saw us but ... well, you know the rest."

"So you knew we were here in the tent? Why didn't you help us?" Lexy fisted her hands on her hips.

Did Payne actually let Brad kidnap them?

"Unfortunately, my guy lost you, so I didn't know you had been kidnapped until these gentlemen here called me." Payne thrust his chin toward Rat and Snake. "Surely you don't think I'd *let* the bad guys kidnap you and your grandmother?"

Lexy frowned. *Would he?*

"Wait. How did Rat and Snake know we got kidnapped?"

Rat overheard her and walked over. "We got worried when you guys didn't come back so we did a little snooping around. We saw Brad and that other guy bringing some really big sacks of beans to the shed."

Snake joined them. "We thought that was pretty strange and after we asked around and found out it was the fireworks storage it clicked in that they had put you in the sacks!"

Rat laughed. "But it looks like you guys didn't really need us to rescue you."

Lexy felt the corners of her mouth curl and she looked at her grandmother. "Yeah, Nans and the ladies have a lot of tricks up their sleeves ... or should I say, in their purses."

"I'll say." Snake shook his head. "I never would have thought of a lipstick bomb."

"Well, I hope all this didn't ruin your chances in the chili contest," Lexy said to Rat.

"I have some of the other guys handing out the chili." Rat looked at his watch. "But I better get back there and make sure everything is in place for the judging!"

Lexy watched him and Snake rush off toward their bikes as Wells and the other officer took Marchesi from Payne.

"We would have figured it all out without you Miss Baker," Payne said. "But I do appreciate you helping to speed things up. That being said, I hope you will be going back to your bakery in Brook Ridge Falls soon ... where you will be out of my hair. If you want to meddle in the police business of your boyfriend, well that's his problem."

At the mention of Jack, Lexy's heart lurched.

How long had she been gone?

"Right. Nice meeting you too." She stuck her hand out at Payne who shook it and then she ran off to gather Nans and the ladies.

"We better get back to the blanket before Jack starts asking questions." She tugged on Nans arm.

Nans raised an eyebrow. "Oh, you don't want to tell him about our exciting excursion?"

"Well, it's not that I want to lie or keep things from him, but sometimes it's better if he doesn't know every little detail."

"I agree," Ida said. "We girls have to keep a little mystery in the relationship."

"Well, let's get a move on then." Nans hooked arms with Lexy and Ruth. Ida and Helen joined in on either end. "I want to get back there in time to see who wins the *Chili Battle*."

Chapter Twenty Two

"Where have you been? Your chili is cold." Jack wrinkled his brow at Lexy as she plopped down on the blanket beside him.

"Oh, we were just walking around. Lost track of time," She said, feigning intense interest in the chili so he wouldn't ask for any details.

"What's with your hair? It's all wild." Jack reached up and picked something out of her hair, then held it in front of his face. "A beetle."

Lexy's hands flew up to her hair, fluffing and brushing away any other bugs that might have gotten trapped in there. "It's the humidity."

Jack leaned over sniffing her hair. "You smell like gunpowder."

Lexy's stomach tightened.

"That smell must be from one of the grills in the tent," she squeaked.

Her heart crunched as Jack frowned at her.

"Shhh." Nans saved her from further scrutiny. "They're judging the chili now."

Lexy put her bowl down and Sprinkles jumped on it like she hadn't eaten in days. Lexy didn't mind—turns out cold chili isn't that tasty.

She shielded her eyes from the setting sun and squinted toward the stage. The judges were sitting behind a table and the three finalists stood before them. Her heart surged for Rat who was one of the finalists.

She strained to listen as the judges made comments on each of their dishes. Rat got extra brownie points for his cornbread.

"Yay!" Nans clapped her hands together.

The judges droned on.

"Just get on with it," Ruth muttered after several more minutes of chili talk.

"Come on Rat!" Ida yelled.

"Rat?" Jack wrinkled his forehead at Lexy who grimaced.

"Long story," she said patting his leg and her stomach flip-flopped as he took her hand in his.

Finally, the judges got down to tallying up the votes. One of the judges stood up, retrieving a giant check that had been leaning against the tent wall behind them.

"And the winner of the fifth annual *Chili Battle* is ..."

Lexy held her breath while the judge paused for effect.

"In honor of the late Chef Dugasse, his son, Rick Monroe!"

The field erupted in applause. Lexy, Nans, Ruth, Ida and Helen clapped and high-fived each other.

"Way to go!" Nans yelled.

Helen let out a loud wolf whistle.

Ida sucked down a margarita and Lexy craned her neck to see behind the older woman, wondering if she had a stash of them.

Amidst the din of the applause and whistles, Lexy thought she heard the distinctive sound of bottle rockets. The applause started to die down and she realized it *was* bottle rockets along with a series of loud bangs.

Jack swiveled his head around, looking at the sky. "Why are they starting the fireworks *now*? It's still light out."

Lexy's heart skipped and she exchanged a look with Nans remembering how the fireworks storage shed had been on fire when they'd roared off on the motorcycles.

Lexy flinched when she heard another round of loud bangs and saw flashes of light in the sky.

Jack's forehead wrinkled as he looked up. "I hope that wasn't the finale ... you can hardly see anything."

"Oh, I bet that was just a little preview." Ida giggled, sloshing part of her margarita on Lexy.

"Hey, isn't that your detective friend?" Jack pointed down toward the parking lot and Lexy swiveled her head in that direction, glad to have something distracting Jack from the fireworks.

In the parking lot, Payne and Wells were stuffing Marchesi, Brad Meltzer and their accomplice into separate police cars.

"Yes," Lexy said. "He's arresting the killer."

"So, it *was* that other chef?" Jack asked.

"Yep, guess so." Lexy smiled at Jack.

Jack brushed his lips against her forehead and she felt her stomach flip at the tender gesture.

"I'm so proud of you," he said.

Lexy narrowed her eyes. "Why?"

"Well, you're up here and the arrest is happening down there."

Lexy glanced down at the parking lot. "So?"

"So, that shows you're finally learning to leave the dangerous stuff to the police." Jack took both her hands in his. "Isn't it much easier ... and less dangerous this way?"

Lexy glanced over Jack's shoulder at Nans who made a 'zipping up the lips and throwing away the key' motion, then turned back to Jack.

She smiled up at him, her heart melting at the love in his eyes, her stomach suffering a twinge of guilt for not telling him *exactly* the whole truth.

"Yes," she said. "Yes it is."

The End.

***

A Note from The Author

Thanks so much for reading my cozy mystery "*Bake, Battle and Roll*". I hope you liked reading it as much as I loved writing it. If you did, and feel inclined to leave a review, I really would appreciate it.

This is book six of the Lexy Baker series, you can find the rest of the books on my website, or over at Amazon if you want to read more of Lexy's and Nans's adventures.

Also, if you like cozy mysteries, you might like my book "*Dead Wrong*" which is book one in the Blackmoore Sisters series. Set in the seaside town of Noquitt Maine, the Blackmoore sisters will take you on a journey of secrets, romance and maybe even a little magic. I have an excerpt from it at the end of this book.

This book has been through many edits with several people and even some software programs, but since nothing is infallible (even the software programs) you might catch a spelling error or mistake and, if you do, I sure would appreciate it if you let me know - you can contact me at *lee@leighanndobbs.com.*

Oh, and I love to connect with my readers so please do visit me on facebook at *http://www.facebook.com/leighanndobbsbooks* or at my website *http://www.leighanndobbs.com.*

Are you signed up to get notifications of my latest releases and special contests? Go to: *http://www.leighanndobbs.com/newsletter* and enter your email address to signup - I promise never to share it and I only send emails every couple of weeks so I won't fill up your inbox.

About The Author

Leighann Dobbs discovered her passion for writing after a twenty year career as a software engineer. She lives in New Hampshire with her husband Bruce, their trusty Chihuahua mix Mojo and beautiful rescue cat, Kitty. When she's not reading, gardening or selling antiques, she likes to write romance and cozy mystery novels and novelettes which are perfect for the busy person on the go.

Find out about her latest books and how to get discounts on them by signing up at:

http://www.leighanndobbs.com/newsletter

Connect with Leighann on Facebook and Twitter

http://facebook.com/leighanndobbsbooks

http://twitter.com/leighanndobbs

***

More Books By Leighann Dobbs:

Lexy Baker
Cozy Mystery Series
* * *

Killer Cupcakes
Dying For Danish
Murder, Money and Marzipan
3 Bodies and a Biscotti
Brownies, Bodies & Bad Guys
Wedded Blintz

Blackmoore Sisters
Cozy Mystery Series
* * *

Dead Wrong
Dead & Buried
Dead Tide
Buried Secrets

Contemporary
Romance
* * *

Sweet Escapes
Reluctant Romance

Excerpt From Dead Wrong:

Morgan Blackmoore tapped her finger lightly on the counter, her mind barely registering the low buzz of voices behind her in the crowded coffee shop as she mentally prioritized the tasks that awaited her back at her own store.

"Here you go, one yerba mate tea and a vanilla latte." Felicity rang up the purchase, as Morgan dug in the front pocket of her faded denim jeans for some cash which she traded for the two paper cups.

Inhaling the spicy aroma of the tea, she turned to leave, her long, silky black hair swinging behind her. Elbowing her way through the crowd, she headed toward the door. At this time of morning, the coffee shop was filled with locals and Morgan knew almost all of them well enough to exchange a quick greeting or nod.

Suddenly a short, stout figure appeared, blocking her path. Morgan let out a sharp breath, recognizing the figure as Prudence Littlefield.

Prudence had a long running feud with the Blackmoore's which dated back to some sort of run-in she'd had with Morgan's grandmother when they were young girls. As a result, Prudence loved to harass and berate the Blackmoore girls in public. Morgan's eyes darted around the room, looking for an escape route.

"Just who do you think you are?" Prudence demanded, her hands fisted on her hips, legs spaced shoulder width apart. Morgan noticed she was wearing her usual knee high rubber boots and an orange sunflower scarf.

Morgan's brow furrowed over her ice blue eyes as she stared at the older woman's prune like face.

"Excuse me?"

"Don't you play dumb with me Morgan Blackmoore. What kind of concoction did you give my Ed? He's been acting plumb crazy."

Morgan thought back over the previous week's customers. Ed Littlefield *had* come into her herbal remedies shop, but she'd be damned if she'd announce to the whole town what he was after.

She narrowed her eyes at Prudence. "That's between me and Ed."

Prudence's cheeks turned crimson. Her nostrils flared. "You know what *I* think," she said narrowing her eyes and leaning in toward Morgan, "I think you're a witch, just like your great-great-great-grandmother!"

Morgan felt an angry heat course through her veins. There was nothing she hated more than being called a witch. She was a Doctor of Pharmacology with a Master Herbalist's license, not some sort of spell-casting conjurer.

The coffee shop had grown silent. Morgan could feel the crowd staring at her. She leaned forward, looking wrinkled old Prudence Littlefield straight in the eye.

"Well now, I think we know that's not true," she said, her voice barely above a whisper,

"Because if I was a witch, I'd have turned you into a newt long ago."

Then she pushed her way past the old crone and fled out the coffee shop door.

***

Fiona Blackmoore stared at the amethyst crystal in front of her wondering how to work it into a pendant. On most days, she could easily figure out exactly how to cut and position the stone, but right now her brain was in a pre-caffeine fog.

Where was Morgan with her latte?

She sighed, looking at her watch. It was ten past eight, Morgan should be here by now, she thought impatiently.

Fiona looked around the small shop, *Sticks and Stones*, she shared with her sister. An old cottage that had been in the family for generations, it sat at one of the highest points in their town of Noquitt, Maine.

Turning in her chair, she looked out the back window. In between the tree trunks that made up a small patch of woods, she had a bird's eye view of the sparkling, sapphire blue Atlantic Ocean in the distance.

The cottage sat about 500 feet inland at the top of a high cliff that plunged into the Atlantic. If the woods were cleared, like the developers wanted, the view would be even better. But Fiona would have none of that, no matter how much the developers offered them, or how much they needed the money. She and her sisters would never sell the cottage.

She turned away from the window and surveyed the inside of the shop. One side was setup as an apothecary of sorts. Antique slotted shelves loaded with various herbs lined the walls. Dried weeds hung from the rafters and several mortar and pestles stood on the counter, ready for whatever herbal concoctions her sister was hired to make.

On her side sat a variety of gemologist tools and a large assortment of crystals. Three antique oak and glass jewelry cases displayed her creations. Fiona smiled as she looked at them. Since childhood she had been fascinated with rocks and gems so it was no surprise to anyone when she grew up to become a gemologist and jewelry designer, creating jewelry not only for its beauty, but also for its healing properties.

The two sisters vocations suited each other perfectly and they often worked together providing customers with crystal and herbal healing for whatever ailed them.

The jangling of the bell over the door brought her attention to the front of the shop. She breathed a sigh of relief when Morgan burst through the door, her cheeks flushed, holding two steaming paper cups.

"What's the matter?" Fiona held her hand out, accepting the drink gratefully. Peeling back the plastic tab, she inhaled the sweet vanilla scent of the latte.

"I just had a run in with Prudence Littlefield!" Morgan's eyes flashed with anger.

"Oh? I saw her walking down Shore road this morning wearing that god-awful orange sunflower scarf. What was the run-in about this time?" Fiona took the first sip of her latte, closing her eyes and waiting for the caffeine to power her blood stream. She'd had her own run-ins with Pru Littlefield and had learned to take them in stride.

"She was upset about an herbal mix I made for Ed. She called me a witch!"

"What did you make for him?"

"Just some Ginkgo, Ginseng and Horny Goat Weed ... although the latter he said was for Prudence."

Fiona's eyes grew wide. "Aren't those herbs for impotence?"

Morgan shrugged "Well, that's what he wanted."

"No wonder Prudence was mad...although you'd think just being married to her would have caused the impotence."

Morgan burst out laughing. "No kidding. I had to question his sanity when he asked me for it. I thought maybe he had a girlfriend on the side."

Fiona shook her head trying to clear the unwanted images of Ed and Prudence Littlefield together.

"Well, I wouldn't let it ruin my day. You know how *she* is."

Morgan put her tea on the counter, then turned to her apothecary shelf and picked several herbs out of the slots. "I know, but she always seems to know how to push my buttons. Especially when she calls me a witch."

Fiona grimaced. "Right, well I wish we *were* witches. Then we could just conjure up some money and not be scrambling to pay the taxes on this shop and the house."

Morgan sat in a tall chair behind the counter and proceeded to measure dried herbs into a mortar.

"I know. I saw Eli Stark in town yesterday and he was pestering me about selling the shop again."

"What did you tell him?"

"I told him we'd sell over our dead bodies." Morgan picked up a pestle and started grinding away at the herbs.

Fiona smiled. Eli Stark had been after them for almost a year to sell the small piece of land their shop sat on. He had visions of buying it, along with some adjacent lots in order to develop the area into high end condos.

Even though their parents early deaths had left Fiona, Morgan and their two other sisters property rich but cash poor the four of them agreed they would never sell. Both the small shop and the stately ocean home they lived in had been in the family for generations and they didn't want *their* generation to be the one that lost them.

The only problem was, although they owned the properties outright, the taxes were astronomical and, on their meager earnings, they were all just scraping by to make ends meet.

All the more reason to get this necklace finished so I can get paid. Thankfully, the caffeine had finally cleared the cobwebs in her head and Fiona was ready to get to work. Staring down at the amethyst, a vision of the perfect shape to cut the stone appeared in her mind. She grabbed her tools and started shaping the stone.

Fiona and Morgan were both lost in their work. They worked silently, the only sounds in the little shop being the scrape of mortar on pestle and the hum of Fiona's gem grinding tool mixed with a few melodic tweets and chirps that floated in from the open window.

Fiona didn't know how long they were working like that when the bell over the shop door chimed again. She figured it must have been an hour or two judging by the fact that the few sips left in the bottom of her latte cup had grown cold.

She smiled, looking up from her work to greet their potential customer, but the smile froze on her face when she saw who it was.

Sheriff Overton stood in the door flanked by two police officers. A toothpick jutted out of the side of Overton's mouth and judging by the looks on all three of their faces, they weren't there to buy herbs or crystals.

Fiona could almost hear her heart beating in the silence as the men stood there, adjusting their eyes to the light and getting their bearings.

"Can we help you?" Morgan asked, stopping her work to wipe her hands on a towel.

Overton's head swiveled in her direction like a hawk spying a rabbit in a field.

"That's her." He nodded to the two uniformed men who approached Morgan hesitantly. Fiona recognized one of the men as Brody Hunter, whose older brother Morgan had dated all through high school. She saw Brody look questioningly at the Sheriff.

The other man stood a head taller than Brody. Fiona noticed his dark hair and broad shoulders but her assessment of him stopped there when she saw him pulling out a pair of handcuffs.

Her heart lurched at the look of panic on her sister's face as the men advanced toward her.

"Just what is this all about?" She demanded, standing up and taking a step toward the Sheriff.

There was no love lost between the Sheriff and Fiona. They'd had a few run-ins and she thought he was an egotistical bore and probably crooked too. He ignored her question focusing his attention on Morgan. The next words out of his mouth chilled Fiona to the core.

"Morgan Blackmoore ... you're under arrest for the murder of Prudence Littlefield."

***

Find out where you can buy Dead Wrong at my website:

http://www.leighanndobbs.com

Made in United States
Troutdale, OR
07/06/2024

21057416R00136